FLAWLESS DESIRE

FLAWLESS: BOOK ONE

ROXY SLOANE

ROXY SLOANE BOOKS

For the readers seeking a dominant book boyfriend who knows how to use his words...

PROLOGUE

DESIRE IS A POWERFUL THING.

People say that it's ambition, or love, or rage that makes the world turn. That sends armies to wage war, and brings empires crashing into dust. But desire... Desire is a force greater than anything.

The craving deep inside that demands satisfaction—no matter what the cost. It doesn't matter if you're begging for surrender or aching for control. Dreaming of the hot slide of friction, lips parted in a desperate gasp of pleasure.

Desire will make a fool of you.

You feel it now, don't you? Your heart beating faster, that shiver of lust curling down your spine. Your nipples tighten into stiff peaks, aching, as that tell-tale rush of heat spirals lower, slick between your thighs.

What will it take to satisfy you now?

A soft touch? A firm grip?

A hard, unyielding fuck?

Facedown in the bedsheets, sobbing with need. A fist in your hair, unfamiliar weight bearing down. You never thought you'd go this far, but still, desire will urge you on. Past reason. Beyond pride.

And it will never let you go.

Because desire is never truly satisfied. Even as you lay claim to everything you've wanted; even as the thick waves of pleasure ebb away, you feel it. Calling again.

Wanting more.

It's how my family built its luxury jewelry empire. Under my control, Sterling Cross has made desire into an art form. Turned craving into a billion-dollar brand that spans the globe.

The glitter of jewels, tempting in the darkness. The cold press of platinum on hot, flushed skin.

I thought I was above the fray. I knew how to keep my needs in check: nameless women in dark rooms, pretty little things on my arm, as much an ornament as the exquisite jewels caressing their skin. Never getting close. Never once threatening my control. Always unravelling under my expert touch, until they begged for more.

I was the master of desire.

Until *her*.

1

JULIET

DO you ever wake up in the morning and feel like today, everything could change?

Maybe it's wishful thinking, but the moment I open my eyes on Friday morning, *something* feels different. The grey New York skies are gleaming a bright blue outside the windows, my alarm is playing my favorite song, and my roommate hasn't made it home from her latest walk of shame, so there's plenty of hot water still left in the shower. By the time I've dressed in my smartest pencil skirt and blouse, aka, the Interview outfit, and headed on the subway downtown, I'm just about ready to believe that fate—or the subway—is on my side this time.

And after the year I've had, I could use the break.

But today, I'm determined to change my luck. I even make it to Tribeca with twenty minutes to spare, so I duck into the nearest Starbucks for a pre-interview caffeine jolt. Taking my place in the line, I try to give myself a pep talk for the battle ahead. An assistant position at a luxury jewelry company like Sterling Cross isn't like answering the phones at the local dry cleaner, so I'm going to need to polish up my experience as bright as the diamonds they sell. Sure, I've been stringing along basic admin jobs for the past few years, but that just means I'm good at multitasking. I'm *scrappy*. *Resourceful*.

Or dead broke and at the very end of my rope.

My phone buzzes with a call, and I wince when I see the number. Meadow View Residential Home doesn't have a view of a meadow, but it's the nicest facility I could afford.

I let it go to voicemail, then brace myself to listen to the latest 'concerned' message from the billing department.

"Miss Nichols? We've been trying to reach you. If you can call me back as soon as possible, we need to discuss your late payments that are past due."

Payments. As in, more than one. My mom's Alzheimer's is advancing fast, and she needs round-the-clock care. Expensive care. The proceeds from selling our house lasted a couple of years, but now, I know the latest bills are piling up—and the facility won't be patient for long.

Which is why I need this job... Not because an executive assistant salary can even come close to covering the cost. No, once I'm in the door, there's a whole different payday on the table.

One that could solve all my problems.

Just thinking about the shady mess I've gotten into gives me butterflies in my stomach and shaking hands. Hmm... Maybe I should get decaf this time.

The line is inching forwards at the coffee shop when my cellphone buzzes again. It's Kelsey, my roommate, who must have finally made it back from her late-night hookup.

"I'm freaking out," I tell her.

"They're going to love you, Juliet. Obviously."

"If I don't say anything stupid out of sheer exhaustion," I sigh. "I hardly slept last night."

"Oooh, that's right. You had a date! How were things with whats-his-name?" Kelsey perks right up. But I just give a hollow laugh.

"I don't want to talk about it."

"That bad?"

"Worse." I wince at the memory. "He still lives with his parents."

"Well, that's not so ba—"

"—And he doesn't seem to want to *leave*." I continue. "All he did was talk about the gaming magazine he writes for. There's only so much *Call of Duty*-talk I can take. And, worst of all.... He's a bad kisser."

"How bad?"

"*Bad*." The line starts moving again so I turn, knocking into the person behind me. I turn to apologize.

And all my senses go haywire.

Because standing there, just inches away, is a wicked fantasy in a custom suit. Over six-feet-tall, with strong, angular features and sensual lips. He's got slate blue eyes, and the kind of hair you want to run your fingers through, tousled and dark.

Or maybe that's just me.

I blush, I can't help it. "Sorry," I murmur quickly, but the guy hasn't even noticed I bumped him: He's scrolling through his phone, with Airpods stuffed in his perfect ears.

He's totally oblivious to my existence.

Story of my life.

"Juliet?" Kelsey's voice breaks through my lustful haze. "You were telling me about your bad make out. Maybe it wasn't a dealbreaker?" she asks, ever the optimist. "You could train him, if he's hot enough. And rich enough. Is he?"

I have to laugh. This is why Kelsey has a date every Saturday night, and I... Don't. "You can't teach a guy to kiss, not so you feel it right to your toes." I tell her. "You know when a guy reaches for you and time just stops? And everything disappears, and it's like you and him are the only two people on earth?" I sigh wistfully. "You can tell *everything* by the way a guy kisses. *Especially* how he is in bed."

And let's just say, if last night was anything to go by, I would be in for three minutes of sloppy, beer-flavored action if I gave this guy another try. Call me a romantic, but I can't help feeling there should be more to life—and make outs—than that.

I finally reach the counter to order. "Got to go!" I tell Kelsey. "Wish me luck!"

"You'll be perfect."

I hope so. But Kelsey doesn't know that landing this job is only the half of it.

Because 'assistant' wouldn't be my only task.

But that's getting ahead of myself. I hang up and order my iced mocha, trying to focus. Wow them in the interview first, worry about the rest of it later. But as I'm striding confidently to the doors, gripping my mocha, someone jostles my elbow. My arm lurches, the cap flies free, and a wave of cold, dark coffee hits me, square in the chest.

"Noooo." I wail in dismay, looking down at my no-longer-white blouse. I'm soaked to the skin, with cream smeared down my front and caramel sauce dripping from the mess, just to taunt me with my extra treat add-on.

I look a total mess.

And I have exactly ten minutes until the biggest interview of my life.

I quickly run through my options. I can't go back home and change—I don't have the time. And all I'm wearing underneath is my lucky pink lace bra, not exactly interview material. Can I find a store open to grab a replacement? Not likely, before nine a.m.

I can't believe it. So much for turning everything around.

Tears well in my eyes. Everything was riding on getting this job today.

Everything.

"I apologize."

A voice beside me breaks through my misery. "That was my fault.

"I apologize. Let me cover your dry cleaning."

I look up and find my day has just turned from 'bad' to 'humiliating' because, of course, it's the handsome man from behind me in line. But I'm freaking out too much to care. This is an emergency, and I'm about to lose it: my pride, my self-control, and my future job.

"No... You don't get it," I nearly sob, looking around helplessly. "I have a big interview. I can't show up looking like this!"

The man looks around, and then briskly begins to hustle me to the lobby of the building next door. I'm all out of options, so I follow blindly behind him, but unless he's taking me to an Ann Taylor outlet, I'm all out of luck.

It's not a store, but the ladies' restroom. He guides me inside, locks the door behind us, and then orders:

"Take off your clothes."

"Umm, what... ?" I stammer, flustered. My cheeks burn hotter as he strips off his suit jacket, unknots his tie, and he starts unbuttoning his shirt.

I gape. This can *not* be happening.

Am I dreaming? Did someone spike that mocha with some hallucinogenics? Because my walking fantasy is slowly undressing in front of me, totally unconcerned.

He shrugs off the shirt, revealing a set of mesmerizingly solid muscles, gloriously tight and cut. He has the lean physique of an athlete who worked hard for it, too hard to keep it covered with a suit. Broad shoulders taper to a narrow waist, thick biceps and just a smattering of a treasure trove right at his belt buckle. It's a feast for the eyes. I can't look away, even if I wanted to.

I don't want to. That's a buffet I could happily gaze at for hours. *Days*, even.

"You can do something with this, right?"

Oh, yes. I can. Many things.

It takes me a moment to realize he's holding his shirt out. It's only when one corner of his lip curls up in a knowing smile that I finally get it. He's offering me a replacement for my ruined blouse

I take it from him. "But what about you?"

He shrugs. Like handing over fine Italian linen is no big deal. And to him, it probably isn't. "I'll manage. You clearly have someplace important to be."

For a moment, I can't recall where. My blood pulses.

Then it hits me. If I don't get a move on, I'm going to be terribly late for my job interview. And yet, I can't seem to convince my eyes to get with the picture. All they want to do is drink him in.

And the rest of my body... Well, it wants to do a whole lot more.

I feel a shiver of sexual awareness, my nipples tightening. The man's smirk grows wider, and I realize, he can see the stiff peaks, right through my wet shirt.

My cheeks burn hotter. "Turn around," I snap, embarrassed.

He does it, so I quickly yank the ruined blouse over my head and start buttoning his shirt up. But I'm just tucking it into my skirt when I catch sight of him in the mirror, his eyes on my reflection.

I gasp. He was watching me undress the whole time!

"So much for chivalry," I say pointedly, trying to hide my embarrassment.

And giving thanks that I wore a good bra.

The man turns to face me again as I straighten up. "I just gave you the shirt off my back," he says, sounding amused as he shrugs on his jacket again.

"Right. Thanks," I blurt. Glancing at my reflection, I can see, he really did just save the day. His shirt is oversized in a cool, stylish way, and I might even look better than I did in my sale-rack blouse. "Well... I should go."

"Wait."

He doesn't block my path, but somehow, I find myself pressed up against six feet of taut, toned muscle.

"Wha—"

My question is cut short as he takes me in his arms, pushes me firmly back against the sink, and kisses the living daylights out of me.

Holy shit!

His mouth is demanding, hot and hungry as his hands grip my waist, pinning me in place. My brain short-circuits. One minute, I'm wondering if I buttoned this thing right, and the next...

The next, I'm in sensory overload.

He eases my lips open and slides his tongue deep into my mouth. My legs give way. Heat rushes through me, tightening at my core, and I have to grip his lapels and hold on for dear life as he kisses, and probes, and *undoes me* with his mouth.

Oh my God.

I can't get enough. It's hot, and wild, and totally overwhelming, and I arch up against him, eagerly reaching to—

He releases me.

Just as quickly as it started, the kiss is over. I blink at him in disbelief, my heart pounding, my blood boiling from his touch. I'm unraveled, but the man looks totally unaffected as he gives me a smug grin.

"You can tell *everything* by the way someone kisses," he says, smirking. "*Especially* how they are in bed."

And then he saunters out, leaving me reeling there alone in the restroom.

He heard me!

I recognize the words, and let out a groan. He was listening to my conversation with Kelsey, back there in line at the coffee shop. All my blabbering about my date, and the job interview. What must he think of me?

Enough to land the hands-down best kiss of your life.

Good point.

And if the kiss was that good, sex with him would be...

Nope! I can't be thinking about this right now. I grab my bag and hightail it across the street, trying to put that weird and wonderful encounter behind me and focus on what really matters right now:

Landing this job.

I TAKE a deep breath as I approach the building, windows gleaming in the morning sun. Sterling Cross is *the* most exclusive luxury jewelry company in the world, crafting the kind of exquisite creations that adorn movie stars and royalty, with waiting lists a mile long. Their headquarters here in New York is like a work of art on its own. When I take the elevator up to the fifteenth floor, the doors open on an incredible atrium sparkling like one of their priceless jewels, all light and crystal, with display cases showcasing gorgeous necklaces, and stunning prints of their gems.

This place screams style and exclusivity. Mere mortals not invited.

Except I am, today.

I approach the front desk. "Hello, I'm Juliet Nichols, here to interview for the executive assistant position?"

The terrifyingly chic blonde barely glances at me. "To your left. Wait with the others."

I follow her directions to a packed waiting area, full of equally stylish-looking people. I find a spare corner of a bench to wait, and try to get my head in the game, but it's impossible with my heart still racing and my whole body alive with adrenaline after that kiss.

Who was he?

I fan my face with a copy of *Fortune* magazine, and listen to the young man beside me mutter to himself.

"Founded in 1945 when Levi Sterling fled Europe... Originally a watch-mending business... partnership with Charles Cross expanded into jewelry..."

I gulp. I cribbed the same research to prepare, but I'm not sure what's going to set me apart from the crowd. This is a big-deal company, and the CEO, Caleb Sterling, is the biggest deal of all.

Ruthless. Respected. Even *revered*, if the press is to be believed.

I tried to research him, but the guy stays out of the spotlight. Somehow, he's got everyone talking about him, without actually showing up anywhere. No posed photos, no red-carpet appearances... The most I could find was a years-old PR photo showing a stern-looking man half-hidden under wire-rimmed glasses and too-long hair.

He's a mystery.

I would be nervous at the best of times—even if I didn't have a whole lot more than just a job on the line here.

"Juliet Nichols?"

I bolt to my feet, and follow a brisk-looking red-headed woman down the hallway to the corner office. "I'm Victoria," she says. "Mr. Sterling's *first* assistant. You'll have ten minutes," she says, looking me up and down. Clearly, she isn't impressed with what she sees, because her lip curls slightly, and she adds: "Or less. Mr. Sterling doesn't suffer fools lightly."

Then she opens the door and gives me a light push that I'm not expecting, so I stumble into the room. I struggle to keep my footing—and my grip on my leather-bound resume.

"Sorry, hi! Pleased to meet you—"

I start—and then stop dead. Because sitting on the other side of a long conference table, flanked by serious-looking people in suits, is the man from the coffee shop.

The one who kissed me senseless in a bathroom not twenty minutes ago.

The one who is staring icily at me like we've never met before.

"You're late." He says shortly, disapproval clear. "Sit. Speak. I don't have much time."

I stare at him—at the way the other people in the room are all turned to him, like he's the freaking sun—and I finally put two-and-two together and come up with *holy hell*!

This is Caleb Sterling. And I need to make him hire me in the next ten minutes—or my whole life will fall apart.

2

JULIET

CALEB STERLING MUST KEEP *an extra shirt in his office.*

That's the stupid thought my brain hitches on while I'm fumbling to scoot myself into a chair.

Not that my potential boss just kissed the life out of me. Not that he'd leaned in and basically propositioned me in a public ladies' room. Not that I enjoyed every last second of it.

Oh sure, those things are in my head, but they're bouncing around like pinballs. I can't quite process them. Heat, starting in my core, has crept up my neck, and is now threatening to engulf my entire face. My cheeks sizzle. And all the introductions basically go flying over my head.

All I can do is stare at him. The chiseled profile. The commanding presence.

And all Caleb Sterling can do is scroll through his phone, ignoring me all over again.

"So. Miss Nichols," the HR man, a bald guy whose name I can't remember, says, glancing over my resume. "Tell us about yourself."

I try to pull myself together. There's way too much at stake to screw this up over some kiss.

Even if it was *spectacular.*

"Well, I've worked a few administrative assistant positions recently," I begin, "A financial magazine, a bookkeeper, I also assisted a small business owner—"

"Those aren't *strategic* moves." Caleb interrupts, finally looking up and fixing me with a piercing stare.

"I... Excuse me?"

"Your jobs. You've bounced around a lot." Caleb says, almost sneering. "I would have thought someone like you would show more forethought. Planning. Calculating your optimal move."

Someone like me?

I frown at him for a moment, trying to figure out what he's talking about. I know my credentials aren't impressive. I landed my dream job at a nonprofit in Chicago after college, but I had to move back when my mom got sick, and I needed to be there to take care of her. Dad split years ago, and it's just the two of us. After that, I worked a series of admin and secretarial jobs, performing great—until there was an emergency, or I needed time to take mom to a doctor's appointment. It's tough climbing the career ladder when you can get a call at any moment that mom's wandering the neighborhood again in her bathrobe, confused about how to get home.

But Caleb Sterling doesn't know any of that—and I hope he wouldn't be sneering at me if he did. Then I realize: He thinks I bumped into him today on purpose!

I have to stifle a snort of laughter, it's so ridiculous. Does he really think I tracked him down to his morning coffee shop, engineered our meeting, and then, what, tempted him into kissing me?

Or maybe people do that to him all the time.

Maybe he kisses strange women every other Tuesday. I wouldn't be surprised. Still, I don't like him implying I'm some manipulative hustler, so I straighten up in my seat.

"Calculating isn't a word I'd use to describe myself—as you've already said my resume shows. Maybe if I were, I would have been able to find more impressive credentials for you. But I think hard work and dedication should count for something. Don't you?" I add, challenging him.

Caleb narrows his eyes. "It depends on what you're dedicated to."

"Well, what are you dedicated to?" I can't stop myself asking. After all, *he* was the one who jostled *me*. Kissed *me*. "Expensive watches and fine Italian suits?"

I see Victoria gasp at my question, but Caleb seems amused.

"This expensive watch was handcrafted by my grandfather. It's the foundation for this company," he replies. "And as for my fine Italian suits... They feel rather nice against the skin. Don't they?"

The glint in his eye as he gazes at me sitting in *his* shirt is the first sign he even remembers our bathroom encounter.

"I suppose." I give a careless shrug. "I don't usually get to enjoy them. Us mere mortals shop at the GAP."

Caleb's lips twitch, like he's trying not to smile. My confidence grows.

'He likes tenacity,' I was told. *'Don't be afraid to talk back. It's the only way to make him respect you.'*

Since my resume sure isn't doing the trick, it's all I've got.

"So, tell me Miss Nichols," Caleb says, like he's actually paying attention now. "Why do you want this job?"

For a split second, I imagine telling the truth. What really brought me here—and what I plan to do if I can get the position. But if he knew that...

I'd be marched out of here in handcuffs.

And not the fun kind.

"You're the best," I say simply. "You've managed to take your family company and turn it into an international empire. You were the first to switch to conflict-free gemstones. The first to give your employees stock options—even the janitors. Your benefits package is exceptional, and what can I say? I love a good retail discount."

This time, Caleb can't hide his grin. Although, I kind of wish he had, because when this man smiles… ?

It's downright illegal.

"Anything else?" I ask. "Do you want to know my blood type? Marital history? Credit score?"

"No. That will be all."

Victoria looks relieved. "Well, it was certainly interesting meeting you," she says, already getting to her feet. "We'll be in touch."

My heart sinks. I've been on my share of job interviews. This is what is called the brush-off. The *'Don't call us, we sure as hell won't be calling you'* …

I nod, hiding my disappointment. "Thanks for your time," I say, already thinking of the bills from the care home coming due. And my empty bank account.

This was it. My last shot. And I screwed it up.

But I'm halfway to the door when Caleb's voice stops me. "You start tomorrow."

I freeze. *What?*

"Mr. Sterling—" Victoria protests, as I turn and gape in amazement. "We still have a dozen more applicants to see—"

"Then I've saved us all a wasted morning." Caleb rises, already dismissing them. "Ms Nichols. Welcome to Sterling Cross."

His words finally sink in. I got the job.

I look to the others, who seem just as shocked by his decision. But it's Sterling's decision to make. There is no higher power he needs approval from. He's the man. The final word.

He motions to HR guy. "Get her info. Her paperwork. And send the rest of the people in the lobby home."

Then he marches out—leaving a row of faces looking at me, wondering what Caleb saw in me that they don't.

"He does this sometimes." Victoria narrows her eyes at me suspiciously. "Makes decisions on a whim. But he can undo them just as quickly."

It's a warning, but I don't care. Nothing can dampen my mood now.

I got the job!

This is it. The answer to my prayers.

I fill out some paperwork and wander out to the elevators in a daze, beaming with delight and relief. Sterling Cross, my new employer. I'm going to be working in this building. I'm going to be collecting a salary—and that's just the half of it. Maybe now, my troubles will be over.

And yet ...

I thought I knew what I was getting into. But I wasn't expecting Caleb. I've seen my new CEO half-naked, I've felt his body pressed against mine and his tongue sensuously exploring my mouth, and I don't think I'll ever be able to unfeel it. Truth be told, I'm not sure I want to.

And that could be a *big* problem.

The elevator arrives and I step inside, but just before the doors close, a hand catches them.

And Caleb Sterling gets in.

I press the DOWN button and find myself grinning into the glass, ice-palace doors. Sterling Cross, my employer. I'm going to be working in this building. I'm going to be collecting a salary, bringing real money in, and maybe now, my troubles will be over.

"Ms. Nichols," he says, and I swear that low voice ignites something deep inside me.

Oh God.

I stand there beside him as the doors slide shut and we start to descend, but I can't stay silent any longer. I turn to him, and my words come out in a rush. "I'm sorry. About what happened..." I trail off.

"And what's that?" Caleb asks, a glint in his eye like he's toying with me. "Your disrespectful attitude in your interview, or... Something else?"

I grit my teeth. If he's trying to make me flustered, I don't want him to know it's working. "In the restroom," I say tactfully. "That shouldn't have happened. It wouldn't have, if I'd known who you were... Well, I just want you to know that I plan on being a lot more professional next time."

I expect he'll nod curtly, and wish me a good evening. Put the whole thing behind us, and go back to pretending like it never happened. That's what CEOs do.

Instead, he takes a step closer and gives me a slow, assessing look. Head to toe, his gaze sliding over my body like molasses—bringing a shiver to my skin all over again.

I catch my breath, aware of his presence. His *heat.*

"Next time, hmmm?" he murmurs, leaning in to whisper in my ear.

I restrain a shudder as his breath lands, hot on my ear. "There won't be a next time. It won't happen again." I insist, sounding firmer than I feel.

He grins. "We'll see about that."

It sounds like a sinful promise. A delicious threat. But before I can react, we reach his floor, and he gets out.

I'm thankful for the doors, sliding shut behind him. They

hide the tremble of my body, and the twist of desire that clenches between my thighs, and the fact that I have absolutely no clue how to answer that question.

Am I sure it won't happen again?

No. I am not sure about anything, at least where Caleb Sterling is concerned.

BY THE TIME I get outside and check my phone, a dozen increasingly frantic texts have filled my inbox, demanding to know how it went.

Well?

What happened?

CALL ME.

My stomach flips as I type, *On my way.*

I take the subway to the Upper East Side, and then walk the long way through Central Park. My pulse is racing again, but not from lust or excitement, no, this time, it's with the sick feeling that I'm doing something wrong.

It's not wrong. Not really, I remind myself. *Think of the greater good.*

Finally, I reach a stately brick townhouse nestled between Madison and Park: one of the largest and most imposing in a zip code of obscenely expensive homes. I pause at the foot of the steps, glancing up and down the street to check that nobody is watching.

But why would they? I'm officially a nobody—which is why I even got this gig.

A dour German butler answers the door and ushers me inside. Faint strains of Chopin greet my ears as the noises of the city fade away. I'm led me through a magnificent marble foyer, to a living area the size of my Chinatown apartment, where an elegant blonde woman is playing the piano, her lithe fingers dancing over the keys. She may be my age, but that's where our similarities end: From the luxurious gloss of her hair, to the designer clothes on her back, everything about her screams refinement. She was born into this life, and feels as comfortable here as Caleb Sterling had been in his board room.

Olivia Cross. Co-owner of Sterling Cross—and my real employer, no matter what Caleb might think.

She's the one who told me to interview for his assistant. And she's the one I'll be secretly answering to, all along.

She drops her graceful, slender hands from the piano and gives me an eager smile.

"Did he buy it?"

3

JULIET

"HE BOUGHT IT," I say, relieved that the ordeal is over—even if a new one is just beginning. "It went better than I expected."

Olivia lights up. "I knew you could do it!" She smiles at me, full of warmth. "Come, sit, tell me all about it. Would you like something to drink?" she asks, then doesn't wait for a response before calling, "Soren? Tea, and champagne. This calls for a celebration."

She guides me over to the antique couches, and sits close, like we're the best of friends. "Did he seem suspicious?" she asks, her brow creasing with concern.

"No... He thought I was just a regular applicant."

"Good." Olivia exhales. She must see the hesitation in my expression, because her smile shifts into something more sympathetic. "I know all this lying and subterfuge must seem crazy, but you have to understand, I'll do anything to protect my family's company. I just never thought I would have to protect it from Caleb."

I nod slowly. I've heard this before—at this house, and on

this very couch, when Olivia recruited me for this undercover mission.

At first, I had no idea what a twisted web I was getting myself into. Kelsey was at the fancy beauty salon she works for on Fifth Avenue when she overheard one of the regulars complaining how hard it was to find a reliable assistant. She knew I was in dire straits, so she recommended me to Olivia for the job. We set up a meeting, and I arrived here last week, thinking I would be running errands, fetching dry cleaning and overseeing household staff.

I was wrong.

Olivia wanted way more: A person to go undercover at her company, to help bust her co-owner for embezzlement.

Help her take down Caleb Sterling.

Her accountants recently noticed something was seriously wrong with the books. Every spring, hundreds of thousands of dollars were being shuffled out of certain accounts, only to be replaced a short while later. It was difficult to detect but the accountant said a sign of one thing—theft.

Apparently, Caleb is the only one with that kind of access —and the sophistication to pull it off. Now that we're coming up on spring again, she needs someone to keep an eye on everything he does. And catch him in the act.

It wasn't what I was expecting from the job, that was for sure. Lying... Sneaking around... Pretending to be something that I'm not... My first instinct was to tell her thanks but no thanks.

Then she told me what she was willing to pay, as a reward for evidence that would take down Caleb Sterling.

Half a million dollars.

It's more than I could ever imagine making with my lack-luster resume. Money like that would keep my mom at Meadow View, and maybe even help me go back to school and set me on my feet again. Get my life back on course, after seeing it derailed so completely. All that, and for what? Bringing a thief to justice?

I could live with that.

So, I said 'yes'.

Now, I watch as Olivia twists the diamond rings on her fingers with anxiety. "You don't know how long I've been hoping it's not him," she adds, her blue eyes beseeching. "Caleb is like a brother to me. I've known him my whole life. Our parents ran the company together. But if he is jeopardizing everything... It's not fair on our employees. They're family. If he's stealing, cheating... Who knows what he's hiding? He could bring the whole company crashing to the ground."

Although I may not know what it's like to live this kind of lifestyle, I do know a thing or two about trying to keep everything together for your family's sake.

"If he's doing anything shady, I'll find out," I reassure her. "As his assistant, I should be able to access his calendar, and keep an eye on everything."

She nods. "Good. If he tries to steal any more money from the company... Well, you'll be there to document it, and I'll finally have the proof I need to remove him from the board and report him to the authorities for embezzlement and fraud."

It all sounds simple, but now that I've actually met Caleb Sterling, I'm not so sure.

The butler brings in the tea service, and Olivia pours me a cup. "I'll head into the office after lunch," she says. "I should be able to intervene with Human Resources and float your resume to the top of the list—"

"You won't have to," I interrupt her. The plan was for Olivia to smooth-talk my way to the top of the list, but Caleb beat her to the punch. "He already hired me."

She pauses in clear surprise. "What?"

"I know you said they'd need to deliberate. But he hired me. I start tomorrow."

She blinks. She's a debutante, the picture of poise, so this is the first time I've seen her feathers ruffled.

"That's great." She recovers. "Well done! I didn't expect... But that doesn't matter now." She eyes me curiously. "What did you *say*?"

I bite my lip. '*Frenched him in the ladies' bathroom*' isn't the answer I'm going to share. "I just remembered what you said about Caleb—Mr. Sterling," I correct myself. "I didn't let him intimidate me." *Much.* "I think he appreciated my directness."

"Good! Remember to keep that attitude, even if he gives you a hard time. You're going to be very intimate with Caleb's day-to-day."

My cheeks flush. *A hard time...* I think of the way he kissed me until I was panting and feel a shiver of desire. "Mmmm," I say, gulping my tea.

Olivia certainly doesn't need to know how intimate we've already been.

"Be careful," she tells me, her expression turning to concern. "He's used to getting what he wants. But don't let the charming exterior fool you. He's utterly ruthless when he needs to be. You can't trust him."

"Well, that will make two of us," I quip, feeling awkward—and way out of my depth.

She must sense my unease because she reaches out and squeezes my hand.

"Don't worry. You'll be amazing. And you won't have to sneak around for long. The moment I have any evidence about what he's doing, we can go to the authorities. And you can have your reward."

I take a deep breath.

The money. When I think about that, and everything it can

do for my family, it's easier to ignore the uneasy feeling in my gut.

Even if Caleb Sterling is slimy and underhanded, it doesn't mean I have to be. My mom taught me that. *When others go low, you go high.*

But sometimes, going high doesn't pay the bills.

OLIVIA CHATS A WHILE longer over tea, explaining the different people I'll meet at the office, until she has an appointment to get to. A chauffeured car arrives to pick her up, and I take the subway back to Chinatown, trying to shake the queasiness in my stomach. The hard part—getting the job—is over.

But as I'm heading up my block, my phone buzzes. It's Meadow View again. I wince, and pick up this time. "I'm sorry, I know payment is overdue—"

"Juliet, sweetie? It's Ann." One of the nurses.

My heart clenches. "What happened?"

"Just so you know, everything's fine now."

Now. Meaning they weren't, before.

"Your mother had a bit of a spell. She started looking for someone named Bill and crying when she couldn't find him."

The knot pulls tighter. "Bill. My father."

"Oh," Ann says. "Is he... ?"

"Gone. Yes. A long time ago."

I barely remember the man who walked out on us. This news makes my stomach drop. She's never mentioned him before. Sure, sometimes it takes her a while to remember me during our visits, but eventually, she comes around. Those moments of clarity always gave me hope that one day, she'll return to the smart, sassy woman who raised me.

Even if I know she never will.

"Is she alright now?" I ask, concerned.

"Yes. We gave her a sedative. She's sleeping. But we thought you should know."

"Thank you," I exhale in relief, making plans to pay her another visit, as soon as possible.

After I hang up, I imagine what my mother would say, if Alzheimer's wasn't tangling up her mind: *I'll be fine. Don't worry about me. I'll be fine.*

Like I can do that. My mom raised me on her own, sacrificed whatever it took to keep me safe and happy.

Now it's my turn to do the same for her.

And maybe with this new Sterling Cross job, I can.

THE WALK-UP I share with Kelsey is in a rundown area of Chinatown, on the fourth floor of an old walk-up above a dry cleaner's. I'm pretty sure that I'm going to die from the fumes one day, but the rent is just about affordable, and there's a great bodega on the corner. I haul myself upstairs, and find the door already open, with Kelsey pouring the finest cheap wine into glasses.

"Congratulations!" she cheers, shoving a glass into my hand. We've been friends for years, ever since we wound up sharing an apartment with a married couple who would have screaming fits at three a.m. We decided to move into a basement studio together to get away from them, and have been roomies ever since. It's an unlikely pairing—she's the blonde bombshell, I'm the one who remembers to pay the electricity bill—but she's been a great friend to me.

We toast. "To new beginnings!"

I take a sip, then flop onto the couch and let out a relieved sigh. It's been the longest day.

"So... tell me everything!" Kelsey demands. "Did you meet him? Was he hot? I heard he was scorching."

I gulp my wine. Scorching just about summed it up.

"Come on, details?"

I look down at my shirt. *His* shirt. "He's... Handsome. In a kind of unyielding marble statue way. Like a Greek god," I decide.

Kelsey sighs happily.

"All the women at the salon do is talk about him. Not only is he blessed in the looks department... Supposedly, he's blessed in bed."

I flush. "They talk about that?"

"Girl, that's the *only* thing they talk about." She snorts with laughter. "Who he's fucking, where, and how much. Supposedly, it's a lot. *Supposedly*, he made a woman come so hard, she passed out."

I snort on my wine. "That's not possible!"

"I like to think it is." Kelsey grins.

But what do I know?

I lean back. Maybe it is possible. Maybe there's a whole lot more to sex than the grasping, sweating, and thrusting I seem to wind up with. Men whose idea of foreplay lasts all of five minutes—or, worse, are so determined to make you come to score points that they turn it into a dull Olympic event.

You can tell so much by the way someone kisses.

Going by that kiss, I have a feeling that I would be in serious trouble if I ever found myself in bed with Caleb Sterling.

A little shiver runs through me at the thought.

What it would be like to be pleasured by Caleb—to the point of sheer oblivion?

The doorbell buzzes, and Kelsey hops off the couch to answer.

"Uh . . . Juliet? Did you order something?"

My eyes fly open. "Of course not. You know my budget would be blown to smithereens if I so much as threw a new Great Lash Mascara in our grocery order."

"Then what's this?"

She hoists a giant white Bloomingdale's box toward the sofa. It's bigger than I am. How did it even fit through the door?

I jump up to help her. "It's probably been delivered to the wrong address."

"Then why does it have your name on it?"

I catch the yellow slip stapled to the front.

Juliet Nichols.

I stop. "I have no idea."

"Open it!" she squeals.

"OK, OK!" I laugh.

I pry off the lid, slip aside the tissue paper, and find some of the most gorgeous clothing I've ever seen. And the designers? Prada... Gucci... Alberta Ferretti...

"Oh. My. God!" Kelsey lifts up one of the items, a crepe dress in ink blue. "Jules... Look at this stuff!"

I am. I can't stop staring. Silky blouses... Chic skirts... Professional blazers... And there are shoes and handbags to match. It's like a fairy godmother just waved her wand and gave me the wardrobe of my dreams.

"There's a card." Kelsey snatches it up. "'*I require appropriate clothing. CS.*' CS!" she gasps. "Caleb Sterling. He sent all of this?"

And just like that, my excitement fades. "That's... Weird. He thinks he can dress me up like some kind of doll?"

"A fashionable doll," Kelsey says, holding up a gorgeous sweater that looks like cashmere.

I put it back in the box. "I'm not keeping anything." I say, remembering the taunt in his blue eyes. And Olivia's warning. *He's used to getting everything he wants.*

"Are you crazy?" Kelsey gapes. "There's some great stuff here. And it's *free.*"

"Yes, but it's like he's insulting what I was wearing. Choosing my wardrobe. What's next? My hair? Makeup?"

"Maybe he's just being nice," she suggests. "Maybe he realizes that you don't have the budget for a new work wardrobe and wants to help."

Right. The sex-god who makes women come so hard they black out, who is possibly screwing over his partner, is *so* benevolent. A regular Boy Scout.

I may be naïve, but I wasn't born yesterday. People rarely act this way unless they're expecting something in return.

My pulse flutters with anticipation as I think of what.

'We'll see about that...'

Kelsey throws the sweater to me and winds a Hermès scarf around her neck. "If you don't want it, I'll take it."

I touch the fabric absently. Definitely cashmere. How many times have I wished for a cashmere sweater?

And did I ever think, in my wildest dreams, I'd own beautiful things like this?

"Fine. I'll play dress up." I agree reluctantly. "At least if this all goes to hell, I'll be able to get decent resale prices for them."

"Or, Caleb Sterling will go full *Pretty Woman* on you, fall in love, and live happily ever after," Kelsey says with a grin.

I shake my head. Because if this goes the way it's supposed to, Caleb won't wind up happy about anything.

He'll be heading straight to jail.

4

JULIET

MONDAY IS HERE before I'm ready.

I'm not sure if I'll ever be ready, but between visiting my mom at Meadow View and psyching myself up to be Super Spy, I've hardly slept a wink.

Not to mention all the brain cells that I've wasted, thinking about Caleb Sterling.

The kiss.

The body.

The smirk.

The every last little thing.

I was tempted to wear my own clothes on my first day, just to show Mr. High-and-Mighty that contrary to popular belief, he doesn't own *everyone*, but that would be putting the mission in jeopardy. I need to fly under the radar, and to do that, I've got to be in Sterling's good graces.

So I arrive at the Sterling Cross headquarters bright and early at 8 a.m, even though the packet Victoria sent me said the workday doesn't start until 8:30. The early bird gets the worm, and all that. I'm wearing a gorgeous heather gray sweater dress and pumps that does wonders for my self-esteem.

The price tag was a thousand dollars, so it's no wonder I feel like a million bucks.

That is, until Victoria meets me in the atrium. She gives me a once-over and says, "I see you got the clothes I had ordered."

Oh. It was her.

I should be relieved, but instead, I can't help feeling a little disappointed. "Thank you." I say quickly.

"Mr. Sterling didn't want your attire to be an *issue*." She sneers. "We have a standard here at Sterling Cross. You understand."

I understand that Victoria clearly doesn't like me. *Eyes on the prize.* I reassure myself. What's that they say in all those reality TV shows? I'm not here to make friends.

I trail behind her through the office, keeping up as best I can as Victoria gives me a whistle-stop tour. "This is the corporate office—PR, marketing, product distribution, retail," she says, whisking me through a bright, open-plan office floor, with tons of glass and stylish brick. "The workshops and design studios are downstairs, but there's a lot of running back and forth. Keep sneakers at your desk," she adds. "You'll be the one doing the running."

"Got it. Sneakers."

We arrive at the corner office, which has its own reception area, complete with two desks flanking the impressive double doors.

"This is mine." Victoria points to one meticulously organized one. Then she points to the much smaller one, like a child's school desk, which has the misfortune of being in the middle of the floor, open to attack by anyone walking by. "That's yours."

Fantastic. *So much for privacy to snoop.*

I set my things down on the mini-desk and she hands me my credentials and shows me how to access my computer and calendar. Or rather, she rattles off a string of instructions so fast, I can't keep up.

"Wait. Can you explain that again?" I ask as she's reading off Caleb Sterling's ridiculously packed daily schedule.

She lets out a sigh. "Forget it. It's not important. I'm the one who's going to be in charge of his schedule, for the most part. You'll only have to fill in when I'm not available." She nudges my hand away from the mouse and pulls up a grid that's a sea of appointments. "Here it is. You hit that tab if you want to see it. Got it?"

I nod, noticing he's in an appointment all morning, downtown. He won't be in all day.

I feel relieved. This is good. Now, I'll know when he's around... but more importantly, when he's not. I'll have plenty of time to get a look at his computer files. The sooner I get Olivia the evidence she needs, the sooner I can pay my mother's nursing home bills and get far away from Sterling Cross.

"What else will Mr. Sterling need from me?" I ask, taking notes.

Victoria snorts.

"Think of yourself as *my* assistant. Doing what I tell you."

"But Mr. Sterl—"

"He's *my* responsibility. You shouldn't have much in the way of dealings with him, at all." She checks the time and says, "Come on. I'll show you the rest of the office."

The next two hours are a whirlwind. She introduces me to about a hundred people, in various departments, none of whose names I remember, since she's going at breakneck speed.

Somehow, we wind up back at Caleb's office, where a messenger hands her a folder. Victoria glances at it, then hands it off to me. "These are the proofs for the new collection. Mr.

Sterling has annotated everything with his comments. I need you to deliver this to Design."

She waves me off as her phone rings. Reaching over, she picks it up and mumbles, "Sterling's office. Vicki." Suddenly, her tone changes, honeyed and sweet. "Oh, hi, Olivia! Yes, definitely! Right here!"

Olivia. Olivia Cross? From the way Victoria's kissing up, it's got to be.

Meanwhile, I stand there, gripping the folder. We visited the design department?

"Oh, it's going all right. Just trying to get my new assistant up to speed," Victoria continues. Her eyes trail to me, and she frowns. She covers the receiver with her hand and snaps, "What are you waiting for? Design!"

She points vaguely.

Fine.

I CHECK in with a friendly looking security guard and get directions for the design department. It's the basement Victoria mentioned, but instead of being a dark, dim dungeon, this basement is surprisingly bright: funky and fashionable, all bare brick and steel girders. I pass cozy-looking design nooks, pinned with magazine tears and fabric swatches, and find myself wishing I was stationed down here instead. It's definitely more welcoming than all the polished metal and glass upstairs.

I make my way through a rabbit warren-like collection of hallways until I reach a big, airy studio space, where several people are huddled around a light table, in the midst of a heated discussion. They're all talking over one another and pointing, as if negotiating a prisoner release.

"Umm, hi?" I interrupt. "I have the notes from Mr. Sterling?"

"Oh dear." They all look grim. Then one of them smiles. She's a smiling woman with choppy hair and funky horn-rimmed glasses. "Don't worry, it's not you," she says. "It's the late nights we're going to have to spend fixing everything."

She takes the file from me. "I'm Mara."

"Juliet. The new assistant."

"Ouch." She smiles. "And I thought my day was bad."

I relax, watching as she opens the folder and spreads the pages on the table. I see hand-painted designs for new jewelry —all covered with red ink scribbles and corrections.

The guy groans, "*Fuck.* He does know we'll never get this line off the ground if he keeps nitpicking us to death?"

Mara shrugs. "How long have you been at Sterling Cross? You know he's got to sign off on everything."

"Yeah." He claps his hands. "Listen up, guys. It's going to be a long week. Long hours. Be prepared to come in this weekend if we don't get it done."

There's a collective sigh.

"More diamonds?" one says, looking at the notes. "He's the one who said to be restrained!"

"And look, we're back to the drawing board on the earrings again."

"I thought he liked the Deco elements."

"Well, not anymore."

Mara catches my eye and gives a wry smile. "Don't think we're slackers," she says. "The bitch-session is part of our process. First we vent, then we brainstorm."

"It sounds like Mr. Sterling is... Demanding," I fish for info.

Mara laughs. "That's a polite way of putting it. But he's not so bad. They're just complaining because it's easier than admitting they're wrong."

"Mr. Sterling's always right." One of the other designers says gloomily. "His taste is exquisite."

I trail Mara back down the corridor, to one of the design studios. Right away, I notice a photo of the most gorgeous necklace pinned to the wall. It's simple, with an intricate, sparkling daisy, resting right in the hollow of the model's throat. Simple, and yet... Diamonds. I get the feeling that's more than a year's salary, for someone like me.

"Wow," I murmur in admiration.

Mara grins. "Thank you. I designed it."

"*You* did?" I ask, impressed.

She nods. The girl can't be much older than me. She's wearing a sleeveless ribbed turtleneck and fingerless gloves, and has chunky boots on her feet with paint splatters. Not exactly professional, but with talent like hers, I guess it doesn't matter.

"It's going to be part of our new line. Sorry if we're all a little crazy right now," she adds. "We're planning the big launch and the graphics team can't seem to get a handle on the advertising. Caleb Sterling's a bit..." She pauses, searching for the word. "*Exacting.*"

Oh, she didn't have to tell me that.

I'm relishing the memory of him, ordering me to take off my clothes, when my phone buzzes with a text. It's Victoria.

WHERE R U?

"That's my cue," I say with a sigh.

"Great to meet you," Mara smiles. "Come down and say 'hi' any time you like. We have great snacks down here," she adds with a mischievous wink. "They're vital to our creative process."

I laugh. "I'll remember that!"

I head back upstairs, glad that someone in this building has warm blood in their veins, and not ice water, but when I reach the office, it's my own blood that runs cold.

A familiar face is standing by my desk. My throat tightens. It's Olivia.

Victoria looks up as I approach. "*Finally.* Olivia Cross, this is Juliet. Juliet, this is Olivia Cross, the co-founder of Sterling Cross."

Olivia bridges the distance and shakes my hand. "Oh, wonderful, Juliet. So nice to meet you."

I try my hardest to keep cool, as if I've never seen this woman before in my life. "Likewise."

Victoria stands up and heads to Caleb's office. I notice she doesn't use a key to open the door. "I'm sure he left those papers you wanted in here, Olivia. I'll just be a moment."

"Sure, take your time," she says, sitting on the edge of my desk. She watches until Victoria disappears and turns to me, her voice low. "Anything?"

"I did get access to his schedule."

"And?"

"Well..." What does she want me to do? I've officially been employed by Sterling Cross for three hours. "Victoria isn't letting me do anything where Caleb's concerned. But—"

"Then try harder," she urges, leaning in to touch my sweater as Victoria appears in the doorway, holding a stack of legal papers. Olivia's voice is suddenly loud. "Oh this is so smart! So soft. I love it."

"Thanks," I mumble.

Olivia takes the papers from Victoria and says, "Well, I'm off. It was great meeting you, Juliet."

She sashays off with a smile, leaving her instructions ringing in my ears.

Try harder.

Alright. Fine. Time to push this plan into overdrive. "What time is lunch?"

Victoria stares with an expression that says, *I knew I was right about you.* "When I say things are quiet enough. I'm going now, so you need to cover me."

Perfect. "Oh. I'll probably just eat at my desk, if that's okay?"

"Whatever." She grabs her purse and heads out, leaving me alone.

Showtime.

I wait five minutes, just to make sure she's really gone, then quickly, I make my way to the imposing double doors to Caleb's office and slip inside. It's a truly impressive space. Light pours through the floor-to-ceiling windows that take up the entire back wall of the office, behind a massive chrome-and-glass desk. There is a full sofa, a coffee table. He even has his own sitting area and a wardrobe with a mirrored door. It's all modern, in subdued grays and blues.

I creep into the room, closing the door behind me, focused on his desk, first. As I come around it, I peer into another open door in the corner. It's a bathroom, complete with shower.

Fighting away thoughts of him stripping down and rinsing off, I settle onto his desk chair. Jiggling the mouse on his computer, I come to a login screen.

Password protected. Obviously.

I make a mental note that I'll need to find his password, somehow.

Next, I go for the desk drawers, tugging on each one, in turn. A couple just have basic office supplies, but the top one is locked.

Well, if he's going to leave his office open, he has to have some security. *Especially* if he has something to hide.

Sighing, I look around. What next? On the surface, it's like a hotel room—there are no photos, no framed diplomas or personal effects. It doesn't tell me much about Caleb Sterling at all.

But just when I'm about to give up, I notice something beside his computer. A tiny silver globe, etched with a map of the world, about the size of a golf ball. I figured it for a paper-weight, but then I see the ring attached to it.

It's a keychain. No keys, though.

Setting it down, I go to the wardrobe and slide the glass door open. Sure enough, there are at least a dozen white shirts hanging there, along with a couple of suits, and a black-tie tuxedo. For the CEO who has to change on the go.

Closing the door, I'm just about to head for the exit when I hear it. Footsteps. Coming closer.

Coming towards me!

Frantic, I spin around, looking for a place to hide. If Caleb finds me snooping in here on my first day, my whole cover will be blown! But where can I hide? The bathroom? What if he comes inside. The wardrobe? There's barely room to breathe in there.

The sounds get closer, and I hear Caleb's voice, murmuring on a phone call.

My heart kicks wildly. My mind goes blank. I'm totally busted.

And then he opens the door.

5

JULIET

I AM SO SCREWED.

My first day on the job, and I am about to be fired. There's no doubt. Sneaking into the boss's office and snooping around when I clearly have no business being here? No, there's no way to explain this away.

So, I have to think of something else.

I smile. "Hello."

"*Hello*," he says with a suspicious lilt in his voice that might as well be asking *What the hell are you doing here?* His eyes whirl around the room, looking for some hint to the reason. "What are you doing in here?"

"Sorry, am I not allowed?" I try to look innocent. "Victoria didn't mention that. In fact, she said I could find the proofs for the latest ad campaign in here."

"No." Caleb still looks annoyed, but he crosses to the couch, and tosses his briefcase down. "I gave them to her last night. She probably forgot."

"Whoops!" I shrug. "Then I'll ask her. Thanks."

He loosens his tie, and lets out a beleaguered sigh, rubbing the back of his neck. Clearly, that's my cue to leave, and I'm just about to do so, edging towards the door, when I see it:

I left the bottom desk drawer open.

I freeze.

Caleb can't see it right now from where he's standing over there, but the minute he does...

He'll know I've been rifling through his things.

Dammit!

I swallow hard, trying to think fast. I just need to stall him, I decide. Find some way of closing it again without him noticing.

"Rough day?" I ask casually.

He looks over at me. "Something like that." He pauses. "And how are you settling in, Ms Nichols?"

How does he make my name sound so sexy? I try to ignore the shiver of desire, hearing it on his lips.

"Fine. Great! I've been introduced to about a thousand people, none of whom I'll remember later, but so far, so good."

He nods, his gaze skimming over me again. He looks satisfied when he says, "I see you got the clothes."

I touch the cashmere of my sweater. "Yes."

"I didn't want you having any more... Wardrobe emergencies." Caleb meets my eyes with a smirk. "I can't always be there to bail you out."

I flush.

"If it hadn't been for you bumping into me, I wouldn't have needed bailing out in the first place." I point out, like the memory is just a nuisance.

And not the single sexiest moment of my life.

"Are you calling me clumsy?" he arches an eyebrow, moving closer.

I catch my breath. "No. Not exactly."

"So what are you saying then?" he asks, moving closer still. "Be precise, Ms. Nichols."

There it is again.

My pulse kicks, and I feel a rush of heat. Then I catch the hungry glint in his stormy blue eyes. Like a lion gazing at a gazelle.

He's playing with me.

But I have a game of my own.

I neatly sidestep him, keeping him facing away from that open desk drawer. "I was thinking, about what you said to me in the elevator the other day," I change the subject abruptly.

The glint turns downright smoldering. "Is that so?"

I nod. It's not exactly a lie, I've been thinking about Caleb pretty much 24/7 since this whole thing began.

Thinking. *Fantasizing.*

"And what did you decide?" Caleb's eyes are fixed on mine. His breath even. His whole presence a coiled spring, ready to pounce.

"I... I'm not sure just yet." I glance up at him from under my lashes, and slowly bite my lip. "I think I need a little help to decide."

I know I'm playing with fire here, but what's the lesser of two evils:

My new boss thinking I'm an undercover agent... ? Or my new boss knowing just how much I want him?

The open desk drawer is just a few inches behind me. Caleb is moving closer. Any moment now, and he'll see.

So I play the only card I have.

I reach up and kiss him.

Caleb is still for a moment, clearly surprised by my bold move. Hell, I am too. But then he yanks me closer, and I'm not the one controlling this kiss anymore.

He is. Completely.

His mouth crushes against mine, harsh and demanding. His hands encircle my waist, gripping me tightly as his tongue caresses me, sending a wave of pleasure pounding through my body. I sink back in his arms, utterly lost.

Dear Lord, this man can kiss.

No man has ever made me want him this way, made me crave him, *ache* for him.

I arch up, wanting more. Running my hands through that tousled hair, feeling the muscular expanse of his back. His thigh is boldly lodged between my legs and I can't stop myself rocking closer, chasing the pressure against my core.

I hear him groan into my mouth, and feel the swell of him, hard against me.

Oh God. *So* hard.

It's intoxicating, and wrong, and totally reckless, but somehow, I can't pull away. This kiss is consuming. *Devouring.* Making me clench tight with desire and desperate with need.

Then a voice in the back of my mind sounds.

The drawer, dummy.

That's right! I remember the whole point of this distraction, and carefully reach down to nudge it closed.

Mission accomplished.

Except Caleb hasn't got the memo. He's still kissing me ravenously, his hand sliding over the curve of my ass, gripping me even more tightly; molding me against the hard length of him, clear even through the fabric of his pants.

And damn, is he impressive in every way.

His mouth moves to my neck, kissing and nibbling on the sensitive skin there. "You're fucking delicious," he growls in my ear, and I shudder again at the raw, animal possession in his tone. His hand moves lower, hitching up my dress, moving slowly up my thighs...

It's like I'm lost in a haze of desire, powerless to resist.

Take me, I want to say, dizzy with pleasure. *Take everything, right now.*

Then a noise comes from outside the office. Voices, loud. Close.

The sound is like a shock of cold water, reminding me where I am.

What I'm doing.

Who I'm doing it with.

Oh my god!

It was only meant to be a distraction, not... this! I duck out of Caleb's arms, gasping for air. "I...I... " I stammer, flustered. Panting.

Wet.

And Caleb just lounges there against the desk, looking at me. Smirking that smug, satisfied smile.

Inviting me to come back for more.

But I can't.

I mustn't!

"I'm sorry!" I yelp, then I do the only thing I can think of.

I turn on my heels, and run.

"I'M TOTALLY GETTING FIRED."

Hours later, I'm sitting on my sofa back at the apartment, buried underneath an afghan, stuffing my face full of rocky road ice cream. It usually makes everything feel better, but not tonight.

"You won't." Kelsey reassures me.

"You didn't see it. This wasn't some grandmotherly peck," I say, red even at the memory. "This was a *kiss*. Tongues and teeth. Panting. Hand up my dress. *That* kind of kiss."

Her jaw drops. "On your first day at work? You made out with the CEO? Jules!"

"I know." I wince in shame.

"I'm so proud of you!"

"What?"

"You were the one who said you could tell a lot about a guy by the way he kisses." Kelsey beams. "And look at you, doing your research up front. So?" she leans closer. "Is what the ladies at the salon said true?"

"The whole blessed-in-bed thing?" I sigh wistfully, unable to keep the smile from my face. "Let's just say... He's blessed in a whole lot of ways."

She lets out a shriek and claps her hands excitedly, as if I didn't just announce the implosion of my career. "That's so hot. What did he say?"

You're fucking delicious. Those words have been cemented in my psyche ever since I bolted from the office. I can't seem to get them out of my head.

"It doesn't matter." I insist, taking another spoonful of ice cream. "It's over. I shouldn't even report for work tomorrow because I'm definitely fired."

Kelsey sits up straighter and grabs my phone. "Are you sure? Have you gotten an email stating the fact? Because it's not over 'til the fat lady in HR sings. And this is Caleb Sterling," she adds. "I doubt you're the first woman so overcome with lust that you threw yourself at him."

Somehow, that doesn't make me feel better. "I wasn't overcome with lust," I protest. But since I haven't told her about Olivia's secret assignment, I can't tell her the *real* reason I was out of bounds in his office.

"Right." The way she says it, with a lilt in her voice, I know she thinks I'm lying. She looks down at my phone and her brow wrinkles. "Who's the stalker?"

I take the phone from her and see fifteen missed calls from an unknown number. It's a 212, New York City area code. At first, I think it's Victoria, or HR, calling to fire me, but I have those numbers in my contact list. I notice one voicemail and hit "play."

It lasts no more than five seconds: "Juliet. It's Caleb Sterling. Call me immediately."

My heart stops.

"What?" Kelsey lifts the phone, checks to make sure it isn't broken. "Are you fired?"

"Maybe." I grimace. "That was Caleb. He wants me to call him back."

"Oooh. What are you waiting for? Call him!"

"Why? So he can read me the riot act and tell me to pack my things?" I shake my head and refuse to take the phone from her. "I can't deal with that. Not now."

Kelsey frowns. "Well, I wish I could stay here and deliberate with you, but I'm late for my date." She gets up and fluffs her hair. "Call him."

I make a muffled sound from behind the rug.

"Call him!" she chants again, right before the door slams behind her.

Nope, nope, nope. Can't do it. Not now. Not ever.

Maybe I can just slink away into oblivion, and leave Olivia and Caleb and Sterling Cross far behind. I can find another job that will help pay my mother's astronomical nursing home bills, right?

Wrong.

Sighing, I throw off the blanket and trudge to the bathroom, turning on the faucet to run a hot bath. I've been wound tight all day, and I need to be able to sleep tonight if I'm going to face...

Well, whatever's waiting for me in the morning.

I strip off my clothes and pour half a bottle of my emergency lavender bath bubbles under the water. Soon, the tiny room is steamy, the bath is full of suds, and I even have the leftover bottle of wine from the other night to help me relax.

From celebration to commiseration in twenty-four hours flat.

Way to go, Juliet.

I sink into the water with a sigh. It feels amazing on my bare skin, exactly what I need. I close my eyes, trying to let my tension and guilt melt away, but all I see is the look in Caleb's eyes the moment before I reached for him.

All I can feel is the imprint of his hands on my skin. His mouth on mine.

His fingers tracing their slow, tantalizing path between my thighs.

I exhale in a shiver, reaching lower to trace that same path.

'You're fucking delicious.'

It was crude, but God, did my body respond to the filthy words. I imagine Caleb's hands on me now all over again. His tongue probing inside me, what he would have done if I hadn't pulled away...

I let out a moan, touching myself as I picture us together.

Would he have moved in slow, lazy circles over my clit, the way I'm doing now?

Would he have slid his fingers inside me, thick and full?

Would he have sunk to his knees, and let that wicked mouth drive me to the brink as I begged and pleaded for release?

That final image is too much. I climax with a gasp, a burst of pleasure rippling through me, too gentle and sweet to satisfy.

It only leaves my body craving more.

BZZZZZZZZZ.

The sound of the buzzer interrupts my afterglow. I sit up with a splash.

BZZZZZZ BZZZZZ BZZZZZ.

"Kelsey?" I yell, hauling myself out of the tub. "Did you forget your keys?"

I wrap myself in an old terry cloth robe and go open the door, expecting to find my roommate, or a lost delivery driver.

But staring back at me is the man in my fantasies, brought to life.

Caleb.

6

JULIET

"WHAT ARE YOU DOING HERE?"

I gape at Caleb in disbelief. Not just because the sight of his designer suit in my dingy hallway is seriously out of place, but because just three minutes ago, I was caught up in serious sexual fantasies featuring that very mouth.

"Aren't you going to ask me in?" Caleb's cool blue stare skirts over me, and his lips curve in a dangerous smile.

That's when I realize I'm dripping wet, naked underneath the flimsy short robe.

My face flames hotter. "No."

He looks amused. "No?"

I pull my robe closed tighter around me. "I wasn't expecting you."

"I won't be long."

A neighbor opens her door and scowls at me. "What's going on?"

I sigh. "It's OK, Mrs. Kaminsky."

"Is this another one of your fellas?" she demands. "Because I've told you about the comings and goings—"

I yank Caleb inside and slam the door, before he can jump to conclusions.

Too late. He arches an eyebrow. "Have many *fellas* visit, do you?"

"It's none of your business." I back up, putting a safe distance between us so I'm not tempted to jump him again. He glances around, and I'm painfully self-conscious of the small, rundown apartment, cluttered with makeup and shoes and books.

"Now, what are you doing here? And don't tell me you were in the neighborhood, because I won't believe that for a second."

Caleb fixes me with an unreadable stare. "You didn't return my calls."

"I've been busy," I lie.

"The rule is, you always pick up when I call. No exceptions. No excuses." Caleb has steel in his voice, but for some crazy reason, I shiver with lust.

The man is turning me on even when he's dressing me down.

I shake my head, trying to snap out of my daze. "Since when do I follow your rules?" I ask.

He glares. "Since you work for me."

Do I? I pause. He's looking seriously pissed, but that was a present tense 'work' back there, and if there's even a slim chance I can keep this job...

"I owe you an apology," I say quickly.

"Another one?" Caleb still looks annoyed.

I narrow my eyes. "I crossed a line, at the office. It won't happen again."

I stop when I realize he's not paying attention. He's looking around the apartment again, assessing it with that cool, calculating stare.

"Who do you live here with?"

The question catches me off-guard. "What?"

"Roommate? Boyfriend?"

"Roommate."

He wanders over to the bookcase, fingers tracing the spines. "So, you're not seeing anyone."

"I didn't say that." I'm on guard now. Because if he didn't show up here to fire me...

What is he here for?

"You certainly don't act as if you're in a relationship," he continues, shooting me a heated look. "Kissing strangers in the bathroom... Kissing your boss in his office. Unless you're not exclusive."

I shake my head, annoyed at how he's making me seem. Wanton. Reckless. "I'm single," I admit.

"I know."

"Excuse me?"

"Standard background check," Caleb replies casually. "I do it with all my employees."

"Oh." My heart stutters in my chest. Did he find anything about my arrangement with Olivia? But no, that would be impossible, I remind myself. I only met her last week, and there's nothing on paper to link the two of us.

I take a deep breath. "Look, it's late. I'm tired. And since you clearly didn't make the trip all the way over here just to check out my book collection, and everything else could have waited for tomorrow at work, why don't you tell me what you want?"

Caleb goes still.

"You."

I blink. "What?"

"You heard me. And you can't be surprised," he adds,

taking a step closer. "I thought I made myself perfectly clear, back at the office."

I gulp.

"You're my boss." I remind him.

"And you're my employee," he agrees. "But that didn't stop you from kissing me today, did it?"

He moves even closer, holding my gaze. "It didn't stop you *liking it*."

I shake my head, flustered, memories rushing back again despite myself. "No."

Caleb smirks. "You *don't* want me?"

I open my mouth to reply, but then I stop. We both know it would be a lie to deny the attraction burning between us, so I don't even try.

"What I want isn't the point," I say instead. "It can't happen again. It won't."

"I think I'd like to hear more about what you *do* want..." Caleb's voice drops, sexy as hell.

"Tell me, Juliet," he says, very slowly reaching out and pushing a lock of damp hair off my cheek. "Are you bare beneath that robe?"

Heat rushes through me, pooling between my thighs.

Caleb Sterling, the man who's legendary in the bedroom, wants me. The invitation is thrilling and frightening at once. No man has ever been so forthright with me; then again, were they even men? Compared to Caleb, every male I've ever gotten close to has been just a boy.

He puts a finger on my chin, nudging my face upwards. He studies my lips, licking his own, and for a second, I think he might kiss me again.

Instead, he does something even more devastating. He leans in, and whispers in my ear.

"What would you do if I parted that robe, right here, and sucked on your gorgeous pink nipples?"

I tremble. Heat low in my belly is spiraling outwards, my thighs shaking, and I almost can't trust myself to stand.

"What if I go lower?" Caleb muses, his voice casual, as if he's wondering what to order for dinner. "I bet you taste delicious. I bet you would make the sweetest sounds, coming on my tongue."

Oh God. I know that I should pull away, but no one has ever spoken to me like this. So filthy. So shocking.

So utterly sexy.

This isn't fair. My body and my rational mind are at war. My brain is screaming at me even as Caleb trails his finger down my cheek, down to my bare collarbone, a burning path that promises so much more.

"I told myself I would stay away, after that first kiss," he muses. "I was determined to be professional. But then today…"

"It was a mistake," I breathe, quivering. *Aching* for him.

"Was it?" he counters, eyes fixed on mine. "Or was it *destiny?*"

His fingers slide lower, toying with the belt on my robe. It's all that's keeping it closed. One tug, and it would be over.

I would be naked. And Caleb?

He would show me exactly why he has his all-star reputation.

And then what?

My voice of reason pipes up in the back of my mind. *You'd have one night of wild pleasure, and then what happens?*

I pause, finally thinking clearly again. If I surrender to him now, I would be a conquest, one of a hundred.

He wouldn't trust me. He definitely wouldn't keep me around in the office.

And my chance of security—of my mom's future—would be gone.

"No."

I pull away, my voice emerging stronger this time. "No, this can't happen. I'm sorry if I gave you the wrong impression, but this job matters to me. I won't jeopardize it by crossing the line with you."

Caleb studies me, quizzical. "You're serious?"

"Deadly." I draw in another breath, finding a reserve of determination I didn't know existed. "You may not be used to women turning you down, but I hope you'll respect my decision."

Anger flashes in his eyes at the implication. "You think I wouldn't?"

"I don't know you," I reply simply.

"Well, let me assure you, Miss Nichols," he says, exaggeratedly polite. "I have no interest in pursuing someone against her will. I prefer my women begging for me. On their knees."

This time, his crude words are designed to shock me, but I won't rise to the bait. "Then, goodbye." I open the door for him. "I'll see you in the office, tomorrow."

"Tomorrow," he agrees, looking furious—and frustrated.

He's not the only one.

As I slam the door behind him, my legs give way, and I have to lean against the counter and catch my breath.

I can't believe I just turned him down. And my body can't either—it's still slick and aching for him, aroused as hell.

Why does the one man who's ever made me feel this way have to be the one man I absolutely can never have?

I let out a groan, turning to go hurl myself into bed. That's when I notice something glittering on the floor by the bookcase. I lean down, and find a very expensive-looking, diamond-stud cufflink. It must have fallen when he was browsing my books.

Dammit.

Now I'll have to return it to him. And I have no intention of being alone with him in that office again.

I sigh, pulling on a pair of sneakers and heading out into the hallway. He's already got a head start, so I quickly scramble down the staircase, descending the four flights fast to try and catch him.

But I'm still one floor up, when I hear his voice in the stairwell, talking to someone on the phone.

"I told you, I need more time."

His voice is tense. Angry. Nothing like the usual calm, commanding tones.

"I understand my commitments. But this is a large payment, and it'll take planning to keep it under the radar."

I freeze. Payment?

I peer over the railing, just to check I'm not making a mistake, but it's Caleb there alright, angrily hanging up his cellphone. He stands there a moment, totally still, and then suddenly whirls around and buries his fist in the concrete wall.

"Dammit!"

His curse echoes, and I gasp in shock.

He looks up at the sound, but I duck back just in time. I hear him exit the building, and watch from the stairwell window as he gets into the town car waiting outside, and glides smoothly away.

"It'll take planning to keep it under the radar."

I feel a chill. Could this be the embezzlement Olivia was after? I was so wrapped up in my lust today, I didn't think it through, but now I see, this mission just got a whole lot more complicated.

Because there's no staying away from Caleb. Not if I need to catch him in the act.

7

CALEB

JULIET NICHOLS IS GOING to be a problem. And I already have enough of those.

The thought haunts me all night after I leave her apartment, restless in my sheets.

Well, that and the vision of what she was hiding under that threadbare robe. Yes, I've imagined my visit playing out in a hundred different options, and they all end in one way:

Juliet. Naked. On her knees. Her lush curves damp and gleaming from the shower.

That sweet, red mouth sliding on my cock.

Even an ice cold shower can't cool me down this morning, not with that inferno still on my mind. The way she gasped at my every scandalous suggestion... How her eyes flared with desire at just a simple touch. Juliet might act the innocent, but from the moment I laid eyes on her at the coffee shop, I knew she was made for sin. And when I listened in on her conversation, and learned just how naive she was? Well, I knew, I would be the one to corrupt her. To show her exactly what kind of pleasure her body was capable of.

Just how far she would go for desire.

All this, and I've still only kissed her. I would be amused, if I wasn't so goddamn hard.

I stand under the punishingly cold jets, imagining that it's her nimble hands wrapped around me. Her breath coming fast along with mine. Stroking me. *Begging me.* And when I finally explode in a jet of hot frustration, I picture her licking me clean.

And loving every last drop.

"Nice of you to show."

It takes me so long to get Juliet out of my head that I'm late to meet my buddy Logan at the gym.

"Sorry. Busy."

I throw my stuff on the bench and tape my hands, fitting them into the gloves.

"What's her name?" Logan smirks. "Not like you to let a woman interrupt your precious schedule."

I scowl. "She's nobody," I lie, heading for the boxing ring. "Are we doing this thing?"

Logan laughs, and ducks under the ropes after me. He's a private investigator I met a few years back, and he knows how to give as good as he gets. Too many of my personal trainers hold back, scared of doing damage to the great Caleb Sterling, but Logan doesn't give a shit about my status—and I prefer it that way.

We start sparring. Usually, boxing clears my mind, but today, my rhythm is off. I'm messy, swinging too early and ducking too late.

"What's got you all riled up?" Logan asks, circling warily.

"Nothing." I lie.

I throw another jab. This one connects, but just barely. I move in, too fast, and Logan belts me with an uppercut I wasn't expecting.

My vision swims.

"Sure, *nothing*." Logan smirks. "Like I said, what's her name?"

I scowl. He may be one of my best friends, but he has no idea what I'm dealing with. The pressure I've been under since I inherited the company five years ago—and discovered just how much of my family's legacy is on the line. "Less talk, more training," I growl.

"Suit yourself."

Logan lands a series of jabs that leave me reeling—but it forces me to get my shit together, and fast. We circle, trading blows, watching for a weak point, and slowly, I begin to feel more like myself again.

In control.

Because despite what Juliet thinks, this isn't over. Not by a long shot. So, she's turned me down—no doubt feeling exposed and embarrassed by the way she leapt into my arms at the office yesterday.

And rode my thigh, eager for more.

But that was only a taste of pleasure. I guarantee, we have far more still to explore.

When she's ready.

I was telling her the truth: I like my women willing. But more than that, I love a challenge. And Ms. Nichols? She's a particularly tempting one.

So, while she may *think* it's over, and we'll be nothing but professional from here on out... She's sorely mistaken.

And I'm more than happy to show her the error of her ways.

Slowly. Carefully. *Punishingly hard.*

I'm in no rush. I'm going to do this *right*. Because in the end, she'll be the one begging me to take her.

And there's nothing as sweet as a woman's surrender.

.   .   .

WE FINISH up in the ring, and pause to gulp down some water. "Good workout," Logan grudgingly admits. "I thought I had you on the ropes, but you managed to get back in the game."

"I always do," I reply, then I hear a snort of laughter behind us.

"Is that so, Sterling?"

The familiar English accent sets my nerves on a knife-edge again. I turn, careful to smooth my expression so I don't show a hint of emotion. "Sebastian Wolfe." I greet him, faux-polite. "What a surprise. I wouldn't have thought an aristocrat like yourself would be seen mixing with us commoners."

Sebastian smirks, dressed in spotless workout gear. Standing six-foot three, with a rower's body, he's used to looking down his nose at everyone he meets. "I like getting my hands dirty from time to time."

"Funny," I remark coolly. "They look pretty soft to me."

Sebastian narrows his eyes. We've been rivals for years, ever since he made his first takeover offer to try and buy out Sterling Cross. His hedge fund is one of the biggest around; a multi-billion-dollar behemoth famous for cutting and burning every company they acquire. There's no way I'd ever let him take my family's company.

Not for any price.

"How are things at the company?" Sebastian asks, but his casual tone makes me tense.

What does he know?

"Fine. Great," I reply, hiding my unease. "Why? Do you need a new bauble for your latest girlfriend? I'd be happy to give you a discount. Friends and family."

Sebastian chuckles. "I can afford full freight. In fact, I can afford a whole lot more than that... But you'll find that out, soon enough."

He strolls away, leaving me with an uneasy feeling.

Logan comes to stand beside me. "What an asshole."

I slowly nod. "Unfortunately, he's a strategic, clever asshole. He's up to something."

"You think he'll try another takeover bid?"

I frown. "I don't know why he would try it. Nothing's changed since the last time I laughed in his face."

Logan shrugs. "I guess some people never learn."

I PONDER SEBASTIAN'S possible threat on the way into the office, but the moment I step off the elevator and see Juliet bent over her desk, corporate rivalry is the last thing on my mind.

Fuck me.

She's leaning over, checking some documents, and even though she's dressed in a loose blazer and pants, the costume does nothing to hide her natural sensuality.

Every inch of me wants to own this woman.

She pretends she doesn't see me approaching, but the flush on her cheeks betrays her.

"Juliet." I pause by the desk. "I have a meeting, I need you to take notes. Now."

She flushes even deeper. "I... Umm..."

I'm almost enjoying watching her squirm, when Victoria interrupts. "I can take care of that, Mr. Sterling. Juliet is compiling sales reports. Besides," she gives a glare. "I don't think she's ready for that responsibility."

I'm about to overrule her, but Juliet has already grabbed the nearest file. "I'll go, right now!" she blurts, and scurries away.

A narrow escape.

It's probably for the best, since there's no way I could focus on the meeting with her sitting right there in the room. I finally dismiss everyone, and turn to my schedule, when there's a light tap at the door.

It's Olivia.

I relax. "Hey," I greet her. "What brings you all the way to midtown? I thought you fainted if you came below fifty-ninth."

"Very funny," she smiles. "You know all the best shopping is in SoHo."

"My mistake."

She collapses onto the couch and looks around. "When will you soften this place up?" she asks, sighing. "It looks like a serial killer works here."

"Good. They can look upon my works, ye mighty, and despair," I say, quoting an old poet.

Olivia shakes her head, smiling. I've known her almost my whole life, we grew up together, running in and out of the old Sterling Cross offices that our parents built. We even dated briefly, back when we were too young to know any better, but now we've fallen into a comfortable friendship.

She may own half of Sterling Cross, but she's more of a silent partner. She lets me deal with all the hands-on, day-to-day business.

And the hard decisions.

Today, she reaches into her purse and pulls out a wrapped gift. "I was on my way to a lunch date, but I found this earlier. I wanted you to have it."

I unwrap it curiously.

It's an old photograph of our parents: all four of them, outside the flagship store. It was taken when they were probably about our age, before the two of us were born. Our parents had been the best of friends—they did everything together, so it only makes sense that they died together.

The plane crash, on their way to visit the Paris store, was a shock. No survivors. And it'd thrown Olivia and me into something we hadn't been prepared for.

"It's for the anniversary," she says softly.

Right. The anniversary. Seventy-five years of Sterling Cross... We have a whole collection planned. Parties, galas, all to highlight the enduring success and timeless quality of the brand.

But what we don't say, is that it's a sadder anniversary for us, too. Five years since the plane crash that changed everything.

I set the photo down, staring into the eyes of my father. He looks so damn sure of himself. I wish I could say the same. "Thank you for this."

"I can't believe it..." she looks around. "Seventy-five years. It feels like the end of an era."

"The beginning of a new one," I correct her.

"Maybe..." She pauses. "Unless you've thought any more about the offer."

I frown.

"From Sebastian Wolfe," she adds.

I scowl. "I told you, selling is not an option."

"Even with the company valued so highly?" she counters, but I've heard all the arguments before. She's brought up selling a few times, over the years, but it's a non-starter with me. Our families left us this company. They trusted it to us. "There's no way I'm selling. At any price."

"Right. Of course." Olivia smiles again. "Always a strong hand..."

Her gaze catches mine, and I could swear her smile turns flirty. But I must be mistaken. Anything romantic between us is ancient history.

I stand. "Thanks for coming by. I should get back to it."

"Naturally." She follows me out, her eyes going to the empty desk outside. "How's your new assistant working out?"

"Fine," I reply vaguely.

Infuriating, more like.

"Good. It's been too busy for poor Vicki for too long. Well, I've got to go." She lands an air kiss on my cheek. "See you soon!"

She sweeps out the door, and I turn back, landing on the photo on my desk. I look at it again, taking in the happy faces, and the excitement clear in the air. My father, the man with all the ambition. The big dreams of making Sterling Cross a global brand.

I idealized him. I respected him.

I had no idea what he was hiding from us all.

What the hell were you thinking, Dad, leaving me this mess to fix?

8

JULIET

AFTER AN EXHAUSTING DAY at the office, I make the trip out of the city to see my mom at Meadow View. A part of me hopes that it'll take my mind off things, but even when I'm far away from the Sterling Cross building, walking down the soothing, pastel-colored halls of the rest home, I can't stop thinking about Caleb Sterling. I only saw him once today, thanks to my quick reflexes. But that one time was more than enough to remind me:

I'm in over my head.

And what about tomorrow? And the next day? I can't keep diving down the hallway or into a conference room whenever he shows his face. That's not exactly in my job description, and Victoria already hates me, as it is. She looked like she wanted to kill me when Caleb came out and asked *me* to take notes for his meeting.

I sigh.

Sooner or later, I'm going to have to face him. And not throw myself into his arms.

When I get to my mother's room, she's sitting by the

window, staring out—at the brick wall. I wish I could get a better view for her, she always loved spending time in the garden, but this small, basic room is as much as I could afford.

And even now, I'm running late on payment.

Still, I made it as cheerful as I could, with a brightly colored quilt, her favorite books, and a comfortable chair.

I kiss the top of her head and sit down beside her. "Hi, Mom!"

She only glances at me for a moment. The look in her eyes, sadly, is one I've started to get used to. It's blank. I'm as interesting to her as that brick wall. And she recognizes me even less.

It's a sad fact of this disease that the mom I knew and love is slipping away, faster every day.

I get glimpses of her, every so often, on her good days.

But apparently, this isn't one of them.

I bite back my disappointment. "Look what I got you," I say, reaching into my bag. I pull out a couple of bear claws that I got at the corner bakery. They're her favorite. I hold one out, but when mom looks up again, she frowns at me.

"What do you want?" Her voice rises in confusion.

"It's alright," I try to soothe her. "I just brought you a snack."

She blinks. "Do you work here?"

"No," I answer sadly. "I'm just visiting."

She looks away, dismissing me. "I don't need anything."

Her voice is so distant, my heart aches. This is the woman who spent every day of my childhood telling me how much she loved me... And now some days, she doesn't even know who I am. Sometimes, she'll let me read to her, or talk for a while as if I'm one of the staff, but I guess today isn't one of them.

"I'll just leave these here," I tell her softly, placing the pastries on the table. "In case you get hungry later."

I slip out, and head back down the hallway.

My phone buzzes; it's a message from Olivia.

'Meet me tonight at 7.' It's an address in my neighborhood. Clearly, if she's making the trek to me, she's eager for an update.

But what am I going to tell her? *'Sorry, I started snooping... And then got waylaid by an epic kiss.'*?

"Maybe she'll remember you next time."

I look up to find the nurse, Joanie, approaching. I nod and put my phone away. "I hope so."

She taps mom's door, and leans inside. "Hello, LeAnne, why don't we take you into the garden for a little bit? It's a nice evening. Getting warmer out there, and I know how you love those flowers."

My mom's eyes light up. "Yes. Thank you, Joanie, I'd like that."

Joanie helps her to her feet, and guides her out, and I try not to feel hurt that mom remembers her—and not me. I'm lucky there are nurses like Joanie here, people to care for her in a way that I can't, not anymore.

I just wish she had smiled at me like that.

BACK IN THE CITY, I arrive at the tea shop in time to meet Olivia.

I think of her instruction to *try harder, and my stomach tightens in a knot.* The only thing I've been trying hard to do where Caleb Sterling is concerned is *ignore him,* but my visit to mom showed just what I have on the line here

The only thing I've been trying hard to do where Caleb Sterling is concerned is *ignore him.*

She looks up at me and smiles as I slide into the bench across from her. "Juliet. Fantastic. I love that color on you."

I touch the sleeve of my sweater, wondering if she knows it's courtesy of Caleb. "Thanks."

"How are things going at work?" she asks with an expectant smile.

"Good." I answer carefully. "I'm still learning the ropes."

"Have you managed to spend much time with Caleb?"

I pause. Well, there's the time I kissed him in his office, or the time he came to my apartment and almost seduced me. "Just around the office," I lie. "You know, business."

"And what do you think?" Olivia looks like she really cares, so I think before answering.

"He's... Like you said. A CEO, through and through. Confident. Capable. He definitely has a way of commanding the room," I add.

Especially my living room.

"Yes, but don't let the charming, witty exterior fool you." Olivia gives a wry look. "There's always an ulterior motive with him. Secrets. Bad ones." She sighs. "I hate saying it. He's been like family to me. But he's the one who closed the door on that, attempting to shut me out of my own business. Stealing. Lying. Don't forget: *That's* who Caleb Sterling really is."

I nod slowly, shaken. I had forgotten.

Olivia shakes her head, collecting herself. "Have you seen anything suspicious, anything at all?"

I bite my lip. "No... But I did hear something. A phone call. He mentioned needing time to get money together."

Olivia brightens. "That could be it! Who was it? Did you get a name?"

I shake my head.

"Exactly what did he say?" She leans forward. "Think carefully, Juliet. This is really important."

I try to remember everything. "He said, "*I told you, I need more time.*" And that he understood his commitments. But it would take work to keep it under the radar."

She frowns. "We need to know who he was talking to..." Then she brightens. "The phone! He was on his cellphone, wasn't he?"

I nod.

"Then it will have a record of the call. Maybe even texts, or meetings..." She fixes me with a determined look. "You need to get a look at that phone."

"But, even if I could get my hands on it, it'll be locked. How am I supposed to take a look at anything?"

"You're a resourceful woman, Juliet. I'm sure you can think of something."

THIS IS IMPOSSIBLE.

The next day, I watch Victoria going in and out of Caleb's office, barely letting him out of her sight. My guess is that she's trying extra-hard to do everything for him, so he doesn't think to ask me for help with anything. He hasn't left his office all morning. He hasn't needed to, with Super Assistant on the job.

How can I get close to the man's phone if I can't even get close to him?

Finally, she leaves his office around 1 p.m and calls back to him, "I'm headed out for lunch. If you need anything, I'll be back in an hour."

I don't hear his response, but she glances at me before heading for the elevator. Are those eye daggers she's giving me?

"Have a good lunch!" I call after her, anyway.

She turns back, surprised. "Oh. Thanks."

When she's gone, I finally relax. The pile of work she's laid on my desk is sky-high. Keeping me busy, *too* busy to ask the big boss for more work.

Not that I'm planning to.

Still, if I want to get a look at his phone…

As I'm contemplating, Caleb appears in the doorway. He doesn't say a word, just hooks a finger at me and beckons. I'm up like a puppet on a string.

For the job, I tell myself. Not because I'm drawn to the man like a damn moth to a flame.

I follow him into the office, where there are papers strewn over his normally neat desk. Plus, his cellphone, sitting right there.

I tear my eyes away. Caleb's busy signing some official legal documents. He stacks them together, and says, "Get these to legal for me."

"Of course."

I take them. "Anything else?" I ask calmly.

"Not right now." Caleb meets my eyes. "Unless you'd care to join me for dinner, tonight?"

My pulse lurches. "No, thank you."

"Are you sure about that?" Caleb's voice turns silky. "I can make reservations. Champagne, caviar… Candlelight…"

"I don't care for caviar," I reply, keeping my voice light. "And champagne gives me a headache."

"I'll have to remember that."

"No need." I smile. "You won't have the opportunity to use it."

Caleb smirks, like he's impressed by my smart mouth. I'm just relieved he can't see the way my heart is racing, and my blood is running hot from the thought of an evening alone with him.

"If that's everything…" I turn to go, but as I do, my eyes land on a photograph on the credenza. I pause, surprised to see a personal touch in this oh-so impersonal office.

"My parents. And Olivia's."

Caleb's voice comes, a new note in there. Something heavy.

I look closer. There are four people in the picture, standing outside the 5th Avenue Sterling Cross location. It's old and slightly blurry, but I can see the proud smiles on their faces. Two tall, blonde people—Olivia's folks, I'm guessing—and then the Sterlings: a glamorous dark-haired woman, and a man who could only be Caleb's father: tall and formidable and impeccably dressed, with a rush of dark hair.

"My grandfather started the company," Caleb continues, "but it was my dad, Jacob, who took the baton and ran with it. The Sterling legacy," he adds, his voice tight with emotion.

I turn back to him. Caleb has a shadow in his expression, staring at the photograph.

"That sounds like a lot of pressure." I say softly.

He gives a brusque shrug. "I'm fortunate. They built it. I just have to *keep* it. They're the ones who made Sterling Cross into the ultimate status symbol... The pinnacle of desire. Now I just have to live up to their name. Make them proud."

I look at him with a new understanding. A new respect. Because suddenly needing to fill your parents' shoes?

I know how hard that can be.

"It's not easy," I agree. "Especially when you wish they were here to help guide you, the way you always thought they would."

Caleb looks over and furrows his brow. He's about to ask me something when

"Mr. Sterling?"

It's Victoria, in the doorway. "I found your driver waiting downstairs. You have the lunch appointment. I wondered if you'd been waylaid."

She glares at me.

Caleb nods. "Thank you."

She hovers there for a moment, before retreating.

"I'll get these to legal," I say, remembering the papers in my hand. But Caleb looks at me for a moment, then shakes his head.

"Those can wait."

"But—"

"You're coming with me."

I follow him downstairs, wondering where we're going. If this is his sneaky way of getting me to that candlelight meal...

Well, I wouldn't hate it.

At the curb, his town car is idling. The driver even opens the door for me, waiting as I slide into the cool leather interior.

It's spacious. Luxurious. And is that... ? Yup, a minibar.

"Sure beats the subway," I crack, trying to hide my nerves. Caleb is lounging in the seat beside me. The car pulls away.

We're alone.

But if I worried he'd try any seductive tricks, I was wrong. Caleb pulls out his phone and starts scrolling—and he doesn't stop until the car pulls up in front of a marble-and-glass building somewhere in the city. Downtown? I have no idea; I've been so focused on him, I've lost all sense of direction.

We get out, and I follow him into a chic, understated lobby. It's all marble and heavy mahogany, like a bank, but there are no customers in here. As Caleb strolls in, the people behind the enormous reception desk seem to bow their heads. "Welcome, Mr. Sterling."

"I won't be long."

We take an elevator down to the basement, where there are security guards waiting. "What is this place?" I ask, looking curiously around at all the security. "Did you bring me to Fort Knox?"

Caleb cracks a smile. "Almost."

We head down a corridor to a secure-looking door. Caleb nods to the guard, then moves into position for a retinal scan.

The door clicks open, revealing an enormous circular-shaped vault, the kind I only thought existed in heist movies. Inside, the walls are filled with shelves and shelves of deep blue boxes.

I've never owned anything Sterling Cross, but I know their signature boxes.

"This is our archive," Caleb explains. "This vault holds the oldest and most precious of all Sterling Cross jewels, as well as our newest designs."

The shelves go on... Forever.

Caleb murmurs directives to a slim woman in a dark blue suit, who nods and scurries off. She returns a few moments later with some boxes and sets them on a glass table in the center of the room. She begins to open them, one by one, revealing an array of exquisite jewels.

My jaw drops. Each piece is more beautiful than the one that came before it. Necklaces... Bracelets... Gorgeous sparkling rings. It's like Wonka's Chocolate Factory in here, but instead of candy, I'm surrounded by priceless jewels.

Caleb sets his phone down and moves to the jewels. I glance over at the handset, wondering if this is the moment to investigate. He's definitely distracted, walking a ways down the aisle, talking to the woman, who I gather is the official archivist.

Imagine, your full-time job, just taking care of these riches.

I edge closer to his phone.

"Bring me seventy-six, and the cuffs from eight-two," Caleb is saying, swiping through some kind of catalog on a tablet.

I reach out to grab it—

And then snatch my hand back, because Caleb is heading in my direction.

"There's so much to look at," I say, covering my tracks.

"For the seventy-fifth anniversary, we're releasing an archive collection," Caleb says, browsing the boxes. "Designs based on our classic collections."

I see him pause by the diamond daisy necklace that Mara designed. "I love that one."

"Really?" Caleb pauses. "It's nice enough, I suppose. But nothing compared to the piece it was based on."

He motions to another box and pulls out the most gorgeous necklace I've ever seen. It's a diamond choker, with a single large yellow diamond hanging from the center.

"Oh, my God." I breathe, taking in the gleam and sparkle.

He chuckles at my reaction, lifting it up out of the case.

I move closer, tracing the stones. Then I notice letters, inscribed in the back of the platinum setting. "'Petal'", I read aloud. "What does that mean?"

"I'm not sure." Caleb shrugs. "The name of the designer, maybe? Or a name for the design." He pauses. "Turn around."

"What?"

Caleb moves behind me, lifting the necklace to my throat.

I gasp.

"No. You can't—"

But he does. Caleb fastens it around my neck. His fingers graze my collarbone, and I shiver at his touch. "Perfect."

I gulp, feeling the sheer weight of it, all those diamonds weighing on my collarbone. The cool brush of platinum against my skin.

It feels significant.

Sensual.

Caleb sweeps the hair away from the nape of my neck and turns me to face a mirror on the table.

My heart stops when I see the reflection.

The necklace is gorgeous. Easily the most beautiful thing

I've ever worn. But what gets me even more is the man I see beside me.

Now, *he* is breathtaking. Raw, strong, powerful.

And he's not staring at the jewels.

He's staring at *me*. With a hunger in his eyes that makes my knees weak. Heat suffuses my body, just seeing the way he's looking at me.

"You look beautiful." He says.

I blush.

"So beautiful... One day, I'm going to fuck you in that necklace."

What?

My jaw drops. My core clenches.

Dear God, but he's good at talking dirty.

"Have dinner with me." Caleb moves closer, taking my hand. "Stop playing these games, and do what you really want. What you *need*."

It's like he can read my mind. There's no hiding it. I can't deny that I want him. My mind's whirling, and all reason is gone.

So I just say the word I know is already written on every part of me:

"Yes."

9

JULIET

WHAT DO you wear on a date with a billionaire?

I slip a dress over my head and stare at my reflection in the mirror.

It's my nicest dress, and six years old—I wore it for my college graduation. Also... I bought it on sale at J Crew.

"Nope!" Kelsey declares, bouncing on my bed with another glass of wine. "Next!"

"I don't have much else," I say in despair, eying my closet. "I mean, I have cute stuff for a casual date... Jeans, tops... That little black thing. But I don't think Caleb Sterling is taking me to grab a slice of pizza in the park!"

"What about the stuff he sent over, the designer clothes?"

"They're all work stuff," I reply. "Perfect for a typical day at the office, but I'm not sure they cross over to a fancy dinner."

Then again, what do I know about dressing for the kind of high-end places Caleb probably frequents? I go and check the rail where I've carefully hung all the designer clothes. Blouses... Boring. Blazers... Too professional. It's not that I want to look wildly seductive or anything, I just don't want to seem totally out of place.

"What about the blue?" Kelsey elbows me out of the way and grabs it.

It's a wrap dress, in a clingy navy fabric. Form-fitting, feminine... "What's wrong?" Kelsey asks, seeing my expression.

"I don't know, isn't it kind of dangerous?" I ask, toying with the tie. "One tug on this, and the whole thing comes off."

"Exactly." Kelsey grins. "That's why it's perfect."

I have to laugh. Here I am, preparing for dinner with a handsome, seductive man, and I'm worried the date will go too well.

"The blue it is!" I declare, and pull it over my head. I fasten the tie around me, and check my reflection. It looks amazing: Chic, understated, but still with a plunging V-neck and a hint of a slit up my thigh when I walk.

"You look amazing," Kelsey cheers. "At least you would if you smiled. This is supposed to be fun," she reminds me. "Try to enjoy yourself."

I nod. But I'm not sure how much fun I *should* be having tonight. Because at the end of the day...

This is an assignment, not a real date. Business, not pleasure. I said yes because it'll bring me closer to sneaking a peek at Caleb's phone. That's all.

Right?

I check the clock. "He'll be here in five minutes!" I fluff my curls, and reapply my lip gloss, but right away, there's a knock at the door.

Kelsey squeals.

"Shhh!" I hush her, trying to play it cool. My stomach is tied up in knots—and it doesn't unravel when I throw open the door and find Caleb standing there, cool and casual in a tailored navy suit and a white button-down, open at his neck.

No tie. Damp hair. Five o'clock shadow on his chiseled jaw.

Damn, this man looks good when he's dressed down.

"Hi," I say, a little breathless.

"Hello." Caleb gives me a slow, admiring smile. He leans in and kisses me on the cheek, and I catch a breath of his cologne, deep and spicy. "You look beautiful."

I blush. "Thank you."

"Ahem!"

A not-so-subtle cough comes from behind me. Caleb turns.

"Hi! I'm Kelsey," she beams, giving a little wave. "Juliet's roommate. She told me *all* about you."

Caleb looks amused. "Did she, now?"

My cheeks flame, but I keep my composure. "I think I mentioned something about my task-master of a new boss."

He chuckles. "Well, since we're off the clock, I'll try and go easy on you tonight." His voice drops, and he adds in a murmur only I can hear: "Unless you'd like a firmer hand."

Oh my God.

Heat rushes straight between my thighs. I can't believe he just said that! The date hasn't even begun, and already I'm feeling weak-kneed.

"We should go!" I blurt, before I melt into the rug. "Bye Kelsey."

"Nice to meet you," she beams at Caleb. "Take good care of her."

"Oh, I plan to."

I MANAGE to pull myself together in the car, and keep my cool, despite the fact that Caleb is sitting so close to me in the backseat, making casual conversation about a book he read the other week, and the new Monet exhibition at the Met.

You've been on dates before, I remind myself. *This isn't some foreign ritual.* We'll eat, we'll talk...

You'll fall into his arms and ravish him.

OK, clearly I need to be on alert, especially with so much at stake. And Caleb isn't some Greek god, after all. He's a human man, bad habits, and flaws, just like anyone else. I just need to focus on those, that's all.

By the time we arrive at the restaurant, I've just about convinced myself that I can handle whatever the date throws at me. "Let me guess," I say to Caleb as we approach the front doors. "The hottest restaurant in the city with a waiting list a mile long?"

"Not quite." He gives me a mysterious grin, and we step inside.

I'm expecting a fine-dining establishment with white-gloved servers and crystal chandeliers. But to my surprise, I find we're in a cosy, cute bistro with homey décor and young, casually dressed patrons.

"Oh." I look around, taking it in.

"Of course, we could always go to Per Se if you prefer—"

"No!" I yelp. "This looks great." A waitress passes with a platter of amazing looking food. "Really great. Thank you."

The hostess seems to know him. Well. "Mr. Sterling! How great to see you!" She gives him a flirtatious smile and whisks us off to a secluded candlelit table in an alcove. "Only our best table for you, naturally."

"Thank you," he nods, but he barely looks at her, too busy pulling my chair out for me.

I sit, feeling a glow—and way more relaxed than if we'd been at some fancy place.

So, it turns out, Caleb Sterling knows how to treat a woman he is on a date with. His eyes haven't left me for a moment. He's every bit the chivalrous gentleman.

And yet I know better. I've heard that dirty mouth of his in action, and it's clear that he isn't all talk.

He sits beside me at the small table. Too close.

I grab the menu. "Looks great," I chatter, trying to ignore his arm brushing mine. "Have you been here before? What do you like?"

"Anything's good." He doesn't look at the menu, he's too busy studying me. "You're nervous."

"No." I lie.

"You don't need to be," he says, and I give a snort of laughter. "What?"

"Please." I give him a look. "You're *you*. Of course I'm nervous. You've already made it clear your... Intentions for the evening."

Caleb chuckles. "We're in a public place. You hardly have to worry about me propositioning you right here in the middle of the dining room. Unless you're into that," he adds, with a sparkle of mischief in his eyes. And this time I really do relax.

I laugh. "Sure, that would go down well with the tabloids," I tease. "Sterling heir caught in bistro romp."

"Romp..." he repeats. "I always liked that word. So full of promise."

I laugh again, and take a drink of water.

See? I can do this. Just some casual chat and good food. Nothing to worry about.

"So tell me about you," I say, once we've placed our orders. "What did you do before taking over the company?"

I'm expecting him to act like every other guy, and fill the rest of the night with a monologue about his life, but Caleb shakes his head.

"I didn't invite you to dinner to talk about myself. I want to know about you. Where are you from?"

I shrug. "It's not at all that exciting. I'm from Leonia."

"Ah. A Jersey girl."

I smile. "Don't hold it against me. I went to school here, then moved to Chicago for a job after college."

"A great city. What brought you back here then?"

I pause. "Family things," I say diplomatically. "My mom... Well, it was better that I was close by. Anyway," I say brightly. "Did you always have an interest in jewelry?"

If Caleb notices me trying to change the subject, he's too polite to say.

"Not always," he replies, sipping his wine. "To tell the truth, there was a time when I'd rather do anything else. Growing up, it felt more like a death sentence, my father made it clear I had no other option but to take over. He had me go into the office with him, every Saturday, while the rest of the kids at school were playing ball. Hanging out with friends. Having normal childhoods." He gives me a self-deprecating smile. "Being a Sterling was never normal."

"Is that why you rebelled?" I ask boldly. He raises an eyebrow. "I may have done a little research, before the interview," I admit. "Apparently you had quite the wayward youth."

That's one way of putting it. Parties in Ibiza. Yacht races off the coast of St Tropez. Caleb was a major party boy, with a supermodel in every port.

Most guys might brag about that, but Caleb gives a rueful laugh. "I made some mistakes, trying to figure things out. But when my parents died... Well, I grew up fast. I realized the responsibility they left me could be a blessing, not a curse."

I see that shadow in his eyes again, the one I'd seen when he was looking at the photograph. But just as smoothly, Caleb takes a forkful of the terrine and holds it out to me. "Try, it's delicious."

He brings the fork to my lips and I taste the rich pate. "Delicious." I agree, and soon our entrees have arrived, and we're trading stories of our favorite dishes from around the city: everything from the perfect corner stand hot-dog to the best two a.m. dumplings.

Caleb pauses a moment and looks at me. "How does it feel?" he asks, his voice low.

I look at him questioningly.

"To know you have me in the palm of your hand."

I give him a dubious look. "Nice try," I tell him lightly.

"You don't believe me?" Caleb leans closer. "Every time I look at you, all I can think is what I would be doing if we were alone... The obscene things I could show you."

My heart stutters in my chest.

"Caleb. You promised." I try to sound scolding.

"What did I promise?"

"That you wouldn't proposition me in the middle of a crowded restaurant."

He gives me a wicked smile. "Unless you liked it. Would you, Juliet?" His breath is hot in my ear. He runs a fingertip down my bare arm, bringing goosebumps to the surface. "Because I think you would. I think you're already wet for me."

Oh God.

It feels like the rest of the world melts away, and there's just the two of us, my racing heart, and the slow brush of his fingertip on my bare wrist, back and forth. Consuming me.

"Caleb..." I whisper, but this time, it's not a recrimination.

It's almost a plea.

"Shh," he says softly. "It's alright. Nobody needs to know."

Casually, he slings one arm around my shoulder, and slides the other beneath the table. "Nobody needs to know where my other hand is right now," he continues murmuring, as his fingers find my bare knees.

He slowly pries them open.

And, for my sins, I let him.

"They just think we're having a normal conversation," Caleb continues, his hypnotic voice in my ear. "They would never guess how much you want me."

His hand slides higher, between my thighs.

I can't believe this is happening, that he's touching me like this in the middle of a crowded restaurant. It's shameless. Wanton. But my blood is already boiling with the thrill of it. So forbidden and wrong.

"Don't make a sound," he whispers. "No matter what happens... Try not to beg."

He sounds so smug, I almost pull away, but then his fingers find my panties, pressing down *right there* against my clit.

I stifle a yelp.

Caleb begins stroking me through the fabric, the way he stroked my arm, but here... Here, every motion is amplified.

Here, he stokes the flames of pleasure into an inferno I can't resist.

Dear Lord...

His pace is perfect. Infuriatingly slow, but applying just enough pressure to make my breath hitch. My grip on my wine glass tightens.

"God, you're beautiful when you're turned on." Caleb comments, his voice so casual he could be talking about the weather. "Your cheeks get all flushed... And when you bite that lip... I imagine your mouth around my cock."

His fingers stroke deeper. Faster. The pleasure begins to coil inside me. it's like an out-of-body experience, except I've never been so aware of every part of me.

Especially the part that he's touching, effortlessly bringing me to the brink with just an illicit, hidden touch.

"I can feel how much you want me," Caleb murmurs, his voice thickening with lust. "You've soaked through your panties, sweet girl."

He slips the fabric aside, and sinks two fingers inside me.

I gasp in shock—and pleasure.

He flexes, stroking my walls from the inside, his palm pressed against my clit now, keeping up the delicious pressure.

"Look at you," Caleb continues. "God, I'm going to take you apart."

He flexes again, thick and full inside me, and it's just too good to take. My whole body shudders with my climax, and I have to grip the tablecloth to keep from crying out.

"Good girl."

Caleb pets me softly until my shudders subside. Then he smoothly withdraws his hand, bringing it back above the table again.

I'm reeling, dizzy from the most erotic, illicit orgasm of my life. I breathe fast, desperately trying to keep it together.

To claw back some semblance of self-control.

Then Caleb lifts his fingers to his mouth, and slowly licks them clean with a wicked smile, his eyes never leaving mine.

And I know, control is off the table for good now.

Because this is a man who will take it. Revel in it.

And God, I will willingly surrender.

"Dessert?"

I blink. The waitress is back at our table, beaming at us expectantly.

"No." Caleb answers for me, his arm still draped protectively around my shoulder. "We'll take the check now. Fast."

I don't know how my legs are still working after that, but Caleb pays the check and hustles us towards the door. It's clear, he has a destination in mind, but when he brings out his phone to order the car, he pauses.

"Fuck."

"What is it?"

"Work." He grits his teeth. "Some important papers I need to sign. We have to detour to the office."

"Oh. OK."

I'm in no state to argue. In fact, the journey passes in a daze. I'm light-headed and buzzing, but I only had half a glass of wine.

Caleb is the most potent drug around.

The car pulls up at the office and we head inside. The place looks different after-hours, with empty offices and only a few dim security lights glowing. He leads me to his office, and tells me to have a seat. "I need to put my signature on a few papers at legal. It won't take a moment."

He heads out, and I go to sit on the sofa, my body trembling with anticipation. I tell myself to relax, even though I'm wound so tight, I'm practically vibrating.

What will he do next?

I've already had a hint of what 'obscene things' Caleb is capable of, and now my mouth is watering imagining what else tonight has in store. Would he take me right here on the couch? The desk? The—

I stop. His phone is sitting on the glass desktop, the screen still glowing from where he just checked it.

It's still unlocked.

I rocket off of the couch and rush over, clicking through to his call log before the time lock goes on. I scroll down to last night, around the time he was at my apartment, looking for anything he called or received.

But there's nothing.

I frown, checking again. It was about nine thirty when he left. But there's no calls logged here between nine and ten that night.

What does that mean? Either he deleted the record, or...

He has another phone.

Before I can process what that might mean, I hear footsteps approaching in the hall outside.

I quickly lock the phone and place it back down where I found it, then take a few steps to the window, pretending to admire the view.

"All set?" I ask, glancing back at Caleb as he enters the room.

He nods. "I'm officially off the clock again."

He joins me at the window, gazing out at the city lights. The view from up here is stunning: New York laid out in a glittering vista, the Empire State Building to the East River, and Brooklyn Bridge beyond. "I don't think I'll ever get tired of this view," I sigh happily.

"Me either."

Caleb's voice is low, and full of lust, and when I turn to look at him, he's staring straight at me.

I flush, desire roaring to life again, wild in my veins.

"Do you know what I like about this place after hours?" he continues. "Nobody's around. We have the place to ourselves." His wicked smile returns. "That means you can make all the noise you like, Juliet."

The way he says my name is my undoing. It's so delicious, like lips wrapped around a ripe strawberry. My heart is pounding as he leans down, and kisses the back of my neck, lips trailing over my bare skin.

I shiver, turning to face him, but he stops me.

"No. Don't move. Stand right there."

He takes my hands and places them palms-down against the cool glass, raised by my head. Now he's standing behind me, hands free to roam over my body, fingertips skimming over the dress.

I shiver under his hands. I'm on display here, right against the window, lit by the glow of the lamp on his desk.

"Someone could see," I whisper, feeling a thrill. Anyone in the buildings nearby could see us together. See him touching me like he owns me.

"And?" Caleb teases me, his hands brushing over my breasts, toying with my nipples through the fabric. I shudder against him. "Let them look."

Oh God.

His hands skim to my waist, reaching that single wrap tie. One tug, and my dress falls open, revealing my inky lace panties and bra.

I hear a hissed intake of breath from Caleb, and feel a rush of pride, and power.

I did that.

His hands turn possessive now, caressing my bare skin. It's rougher, and I love it, pressing shamelessly into his palms. The city glitters below us, but I feel like I'm flying a thousand miles high. He squeezes my breasts, dipping a hand into my panties and testing my wetness, making me clench.

Then he drops to his knees.

My half-closed eyes fly open as he pulls my panties down around my ankles, and lifts my feet in turn to free them.

"What are you—"

My question dies on my lips as he looks up, eyes dark and lustful in the moonlight.

"You know exactly what I'm doing," he replies, lazily trailing a hand up the inside of my bare thighs. He moves between them, on his knees there with his back to the window. Beneath me, but in control in every way that matters.

"I'm going to taste you, Juliet. I'm going to fuck you with my tongue until you're screaming my name for everyone to hear."

My brain goes blank. It's like staring into the sun, the force of my desire. It blots out everything, all sense and reason.

And when he leans in, and licks up, hot against me, I just about lose my mind.

His tongue is firm and probing, lapping at my clit, swirling and circling in a dizzying rhythm.

A soft moan echoes in the room. My moan.

"Good," Caleb murmurs, vibrating against me. "Now, louder."

He licks again, harder, and I sway forwards, bracing myself against the glass as the sensation overpowers me. It's incredible, the things this man's mouth can do. Sweeping me into an inferno; glittering and dangerous, and devastatingly hot.

And all along, I'm exposed here in front of the window for the world to see.

So everyone can watch me come undone.

The thrill shudders through me, Caleb's mouth driving me wild. He circles a fingertip at my slick entrance, then dips it inside.

I clench hard around him.

He chuckles.

"Patience. I'll give you what you need, but only if you're a good girl. Can you be good for me, Juliet?"

I nod eagerly. Anything to keep this pleasure coming, sharp and hot in my veins.

"So ask nicely," Caleb says, giving me a taunting look. "What do you want?"

"You..." I manage to stutter.

He dips a second finger inside me, but just the tips. Not nearly enough.

"Be specific."

Oh God.

He's torturing me, making me say the words out loud.

"Because if you don't want this..." he begins to move away, and the loss of pressure is too much to bear.

"No! Please!" I find myself begging. "I need.... I need..."

"Tell me."

I close my eyes to hide from the shame. "I need your fingers inside me," I whisper. "Fill me up. Please, Caleb."

"As you wish."

His mouth descends on me again, hot and swift, and then he's thrusting his fingers deep inside me. Flexing, and beckoning. Thick and full.

Fuck.

I cry out, loving it. Desperate and dizzy, so close to the edge. "Caleb!"

His tongue swirls faster, lapping at me. His fingers thrust deeper, over and over, and then I feel another slide inside, stretching me to the limit.

His lips close around my clit, and he sucks.

Hard.

I explode. The orgasm rips through me, a rush of pleasure that nearly sends me stumbling to the floor. But Caleb holds me up, bracing me there, trapping me against his mouth as he licks me through it, pulls me deeper, making everything more intense until I can't take anymore.

I break away, gasping.

Holy. Shit.

I have no words. I didn't even know it was possible to come that hard.

Slowly, Caleb gets to his feet, a satisfied expression on his face. "I told you so," he says, smirking, and I realize, that everything he promised just happened.

He did obscene things to me.

I begged him for more.

I came screaming his name.

And I loved every minute of it.

I'm still reeling when a light dances in the office outside, and footsteps come. "Hello?" a voice calls.

I don't have time to panic. In an instant, Caleb is at my side. "Who's there?" he barks, shielding me from the door with his body as he efficiently fastens my dress again.

The door opens, and a security guard looks in. "Oh, Mr. Sterling, I'm sorry. I didn't know anyone was here."

"That's quite alright, Jimmy," Caleb replies smoothly. "Just another late night. Thanks for checking."

"Goodnight," Jimmy tells us both, about to leave, but Caleb stops him.

"Actually, you can walk Juliet down to the lobby. My driver is waiting to take her home. See that she reaches him safely."

"Of course."

I blink in surprise. He's sending me home? "That's it?" I blurt.

Caleb's lips quirk in amusement. "I think we've done enough *work* for the night. Get some sleep. I'm sure there'll be plenty more on your desk tomorrow."

He gives me a nod, like he's dismissing me.

Like five minutes ago, he wasn't on his knees, devouring me whole.

"Fine." I reply, gathering my wits. If he wants to act like I'm suddenly disposable, then I'm not about to hang around and be humiliated. "I should get some rest, anyway. All this paperwork was so boring, I nearly fell asleep."

Caleb's jaw drops. Ha! I manage a smile of victory as I walk out the door. I even manage to make it all the way to the elevators feeling like I got the last word.

Then I realize: I'm not wearing my panties.

10

JULIET

BASTARD.

That's what I'm thinking, the following day, as I sit at my desk, fumbling my way through a boring sales presentation.

Last night was absolutely ridiculous. I couldn't sleep because I kept thinking about him, his warm breath on my clit, his tongue teasing its way between my folds. *Then,* when I did fall asleep, I dreamed of him, on top of me, staring at me with that wicked little smirk, but never quite giving me what I wanted, even as I begged for it.

I don't know how I managed to make it to work today, or to keep it together like nothing happened. But every time Caleb walks past me, he gives me that same satisfied smirk.

The one that says, '*I know how you taste*'.

He's driving me crazy, and he knows it.

He knows I won't do anything about it. He'll torture me and torture me and I will sit there like a good girl and take it until I reach my breaking point.

Bastard.

But what can I do?

Oh, I have plenty of ideas. *Now*. Especially since courtesy of Caleb Sterling, I've been thinking about sex, twenty-four-seven. Not that I'd ever put them into action. Because I'm on assignment here.

A task I'm finding it way too easy to forget.

Victoria appears. "How was the meeting the other day?"

I can't even remember what meeting she's talking about. "Oh, it was... Fine."

"Well, you must've done a bang-up job of taking notes. He wants you to take notes for the anniversary planning committee meeting." She's frowning.

"Oh." My pulse skitters. "When is—"

"It's now! Come on."

I grab my pad and pen and hurry to the conference room. Caleb is there already, he has his shirtsleeves rolled up, looking illegally delicious considering he had just as little sleep as me. He's talking to David from marketing, a friendly guy about my age with sandy blond hair.

Caleb shoots me a hungry look as we join the meeting, and other people arrive. I look away, trying to hide the fact he's been on my mind all night.

I find myself staring at the window.

The window just like the one I stood by last night, as he licked me to heaven and back.

"Juliet." Victoria's hiss pulls me back to the present. I quickly pull out my laptop and start to take notes.

"So, where are we?" Caleb begins, looking around the room.

The meeting is all about the upcoming anniversary events. For the seventy-fifth anniversary, there'll be a whole month of promotion, showcasing Sterling Cross's history, and culminating in a huge black-tie gala. The different departments all weigh in, updating Caleb on their plans and schedule, and I try to stay focused and keep up with the breakneck pace.

Publicity is talking about celebrity partnerships when I feel a buzz in my pocket. A text.

I surreptitiously check my phone.

"I have your panties."

It's Caleb. I feel a thrill. I look up and catch his eye across the table. He's nodding along to the discussion, but the look in his eyes is pure seduction.

Dammit.

My phone buzzes again.

"What would you do to get them back?"

My pulse kicks. I can feel my body tighten in anticipation all over again, just imagining what he has in store. Meanwhile, Caleb doesn't falter. Two people are arguing about locales and he's effectively putting out the fire, all while starting one in me.

He thinks he's so smooth. Okay, yes, he is—I'm so hot I'm almost panting. But I refuse to let him know how affected I am.

'I can do without them' I type back, casual—well aware of the double entendre.

He glances at his phone, and can't hide a smile.

'Naughty girl.'

The meeting drags on, until finally Caleb gets to his feet. "I think we have everything."

The rest of the staff pack up.

"You get all that, Juliet?" David asks.

"Uh... *Yes.*" Lie.

As I'm about to leave, Caleb stops me, "Juliet. I know you're new, but we have a rule. No phones in conferences. You were distracted."

My jaw drops. Is he serious?

I look up at him. The smirk's been replaced by a rigid frown.

So he *is* serious. His eyes go to Victoria. "Did you get the venue suggestions?"

She nods proudly and holds up her perfect list. She even has nice penmanship.

"Good. Start making the calls." He looks at me. "Juliet. Do better."

I narrow my eyes.

"Yes, *sir*," I reply, an edge of rebellion in my voice.

His lips twist, the start of a smile or a frown, I'm not sure, because I vacate the room a second later and throw my pad down on my desk with great force.

"Jerk," I mutter.

David overhears, and gives a chuckle. "Eh. Don't worry about him. He's just a grump."

I smile gratefully at him.

"I should've told you. Distraction is a big pet peeve of his," Victoria pipes up, looking smug.. "He demands one hundred percent concentration."

Caleb is demanding, alright.

I clear my throat, blushing. "I'm beginning to see that."

"You should be careful," she adds, glaring. "When he doesn't get what he wants... there are consequences."

Sexy, delicious consequences, I'm sure.

He's already proved he loves giving orders, and expecting people to take them. As much as I want to smack him for that little play inside, I also want to... Obey.

Suddenly Caleb emerges.

"Are you ready for your one o'clock?" Victoria chirps, folder at the ready.

"What?" Caleb looks thrown. "No. I have someplace I need to be. Cancel all my meetings for the rest of the afternoon."

"But—yes, Mr. Sterling," she says with confusion, as Caleb stalks to the elevators.

And doesn't even look at me.

I sigh. This guy runs so hot and cold, I shouldn't be surprised. And at least with him out of the office, I can focus on my workload, and not his sexy teasing games. So, I buckle down with the filing, and try not to think about his sexy texts.

By two, Caleb hasn't returned—but my stomach is rumbling.

"OK if I take my lunch?" I ask Victoria. She sighs. "Be quick about it. Oh, and you can pick up my dry cleaning while you're out."

I open my mouth to protest, then close it again. "Whatever you need," I say brightly.

She hands me the ticket and waves me off. It's an address in a shady neighborhood on the Lower East Side, but I know there's an amazing dumpling place right around the corner, so I figure, two birds, one stone, ten dumplings to go.

I get off the subway, and pick up her clothes, but I'm just waiting outside the dumpling place for my order, when I see a familiar face on the other side of the street.

It's Caleb.

I pause. What's he doing in this part of town?

He's just walking out of a dim, old bar on the corner, glancing around like he's worried he's been seen.

He catches sight of me, and stops. Then he crosses the street, frowning. "What are you doing here?" he demands in greeting.

"I could ask you the same thing," I reply, sassy. I hold up the dry cleaning. "Running errands, what's your excuse?"

"Just... Meeting an old friend," he replies vaguely. He relaxes, assessing me with a now-familiar smile. "What a lucky coincidence. The two of us. Out of the office..."

"But only one of us has someone counting every minute until their return," I remind him. "Victoria has probably calculated the exact time it will take me to ride the subway here and back."

"Then we better free up some of that time." Caleb taps his phone, and a moment later, his car pulls up.

"What does your driver do, waiting around all day?" I ask, amused.

"He loves Sudoku," Caleb replies, smiling. "Don't you, Henri?"

Henri laughs as he opens the door for us. "Wait, I have food," I say, gesturing to the dumpling place—just as the kid brings my order out.

"Perfect timing." Caleb gestures me in ahead of him, so I slide into the backseat. Caleb gets in after me and hits a button. The driver partition slides up, leaving us private and alone.

I arch an eyebrow. "Now, why would we need privacy?" I ask, with a jolt of anticipation.

"Oh, I have plans..."

My pulse kicks at the possibility of those plans, but before Caleb can show me, his phone ring interrupts us. He glances at the caller and winces apologetically. "I have to take this."

It's a business call, something about East Asian profit projections, and Caleb chats away about data and figures as I sit there, restless. The city streets are passing outside the windows, and I'm impatient, our window of privacy rapidly closing.

I don't think I can take another afternoon in the office with Caleb teasing me.

But maybe it's time he felt what that teasing was like.

I look at him, an idea forming. He's been the one calling the shots ever since we met. Tormenting me. Seducing me. Turning me on.

But it's always been on his terms. His choice where to wind me up—and when to leave me panting.

What would it be like to be the one driving *him* crazy? Making *him* moan my name?

I feel a rush of exhilaration. Catching Caleb's eyes, I reach over, and slowly undo the buckle on his belt.

He nearly drops the phone. "What are you—?" he whispers, and I grin.

"You know exactly what I'm doing," I say, echoing his words to me from last night. "Now shhh, don't make a sound."

I wink, as I ease his zipper down and his fly open. He's already hard against my hand, straining at the fabric of his briefs. I slide off the seat and onto the floor in front of him, settling on my knees as I free his gorgeous cock.

Damn, this man is *huge*.

I've felt it pressed against me. I knew he was blessed. But seeing it up close... My mouth waters, just imagining how it would feel inside me.

But first, I'm going to make him beg.

I lean in, and lick up the length of the thick shaft.

Caleb lets out a strangled groan, and I smile. "No, no, nothing's wrong," he says on the phone, trying to cover.

I close my hand around him and begin to slowly pump.

Caleb curses under his breath.

I watch him for a moment, trying to keep it together. I've never felt so sexy, watching this man stammer and grasp for words—because of me. He gives me a bashful look, shaking his head. As if to say, 'well played'.

I grin back. Then I lean over and take the whole head of his cock into my mouth.

"That... Would work for us," he keeps talking, but he sounds a little... Tortured.

Just like I sounded, last night.

I swirl my tongue around him, angling him deeper into my mouth.

"Fuck."

This time, his curse is audible. I bob my head, finding a rhythm, feeling his body tense and jerk under my touch.

I feel powerful. *Invincible.* And so close to making Caleb Sterling lose control. I rise up, then slide my lips down his shaft again, swirling my tongue as I go. I can hear his breathing growing labored, I can tell, he's close to the edge.

But before I can get him there, Caleb suddenly stops me.

"We'll circle back next week," he says into the phone, hanging up. Then he pulls me up, out of his lap.

"So soon?" I ask, eying his straining dick.

He lets out a ragged chuckle. "I think you've gone far enough. In fact, you'll be punished later for your insubordination."

I smirk, still feeling power like a drug in my veins. "It looks like you're the one who's punishing yourself," I reply. "All wound up and no place to go. Or, come."

He forces his cock back into his pants. "Not here." Caleb zips up, then gives me a look of dark-eyed promise. "When I come, it's not going to be in your mouth, or on those magnificent breasts of yours," he says, all steel and icy determination again. "No, I'm going to be buried to the hilt in your slick cunt, and I won't settle for anything less."

He opens the door, and I realize, the car came to a stop long ago. Caleb climbs out smoothly, leaving me panting there in the backseat.

So much for taking control. Caleb has proven beyond a doubt, he's a man who'll never give it up.

And damn, if I don't love it that way.

11

JULIET

AND I THOUGHT my mind was running wild before.

Now, when we get back to work and Caleb heads purposefully into his office, caring more about his work than me, I have to wonder.

What, exactly, did he mean by *punishment*?

And can he show me as soon as freaking possible?

But Caleb seems entirely unaffected by our little *triste*. He strides in and out of meetings, and doesn't so much as look at me. Not that I could meet his eyes without remembering how it felt to be there on my knees, driving him wild.

By the time the day ends and Victoria and the rest of the staff leave, I'm more impatient than ever.

Ready to pick up where we left off.

Eager for Caleb to finish what we started—in more ways than one.

I linger by my desk, pretending to finish up some work. But really, I'm waiting for him. Then, finally, Caleb emerges from his office...

And he's wearing a tuxedo.

Now that really isn't fair.

I try not to swoon over the sight of him all dressed up. "Heading somewhere special?" I ask, playing it casual.

"No. I usually dress like this when I'm headed home." He smirks. "A last-minute invitation to a charity event." He pauses, straightening his cuffs. "Come with me."

I look down at my slacks and sweater. "I'm not exactly dressed for the occasion."

"So," Caleb smiles. "We'll get you a dress on the way."

I have to laugh at that.

"What?" he asks, looking curious.

"Nothing, it's just... We occupy very different realities," I say wryly, following him down the hall. "Only you could assume it's possible to acquire a formal dress with zero notice at eight o'clock on a Thursday night."

Caleb chuckles. "Maybe I'm just an optimist."

"Or maybe you're used to having the world revolve around you," I tease.

He frowns. "Is that what you think?"

"No. I mean, yes," I correct myself, smiling. "But it's not a bad thing. It's kind of incredible to witness up close, that's all. I *don't* live in that reality."

That was for sure.

Caleb looks thoughtful on the drive, and I wonder if I said something wrong. Then we pull up outside a chic boutique, one of those places with white walls and minimal racks filled with one-of-a-kind pieces. I look through the storefront but don't see anyone. The lights are off. "I think it's closed."

"It's open for me." He reaches for the door handle. Sure enough, he's right.

"Mr. Sterling!" The female associates greet him with giddy, glowing smiles and a lot of fawning. "What can we do for you this time?"

This time... So, I'm not the first woman he's dressed here, I can tell they want to be in my place. Just for one night.

Maybe that's what this is for me, too. One night.

But perhaps that wouldn't be so bad. One night with Caleb to get it out of my system, and then I can focus on the real purpose of my job.

Inside, I know I can't afford a single thing in the place—it's all so beautiful, I'm afraid to touch. But Caleb doesn't browse. He stalks to a rack, pulls out a bright red, Julia Roberts-in-Pretty Woman dress, and hands it to me. "This is the one."

The associates guide me to a dressing room. I squeeze into the poured-on, off-the-shoulder gown, and sigh at my reflection in the mirror.

Some wise woman once said Caleb's taste was exquisite, and she's right. The cut of the dress accentuates my curves, and the color brings out the rich tones in my brown hair. I look like a different person. I'm not wallflower Juliet Nichols. I'm me, just... More.

More confident. More elegant.

And sexy as hell.

The associates give me a pair of delicate strappy heels that are just my size. Still, when I step out of the dressing room, I feel a flicker of nerves. I'm so far out of my comfort zone, I can't see it for miles.

"Well?" I strike an awkward pose. "What do you think?"

There's silence. I look up to check Caleb's expression.

And the look on his face tells me that the dress is just right.

I smile. He's gazing at me with a hungry look in his eyes, but it's more than just lust. There's something else there too. A kind of reverence, like I'm a stunning painting, or a work of art.

No man has ever looked at me this way.

"It's perfect," he says, getting to his feet. "*You're* perfect. Except for one last thing..."

He moves closer, and reaches into his breast pocket, withdrawing a slim leather case. He pops it open, revealing...

"Oh my God." I gasp. It's the necklace from the vault, the diamond choker with the incredible pendant. "Caleb, I can't wear that."

"You can, and you will."

He fastens it around my neck, and smooths my hair back into place. "There, *now* you're ready."

It's not until we're pulling up outside the Museum of Modern Art that I think to ask: "What is this event all about?"

He gives a shrug. "Bullshit."

"I thought you said it's for charity."

He gives a rueful smile. "The charity's not bullshit. The event is. Just another excuse for the same society people to flaunt and congratulate themselves. I usually don't get into it, I leave this stuff for Olivia But this one, I'm told, is unavoidable. I have to make an appearance."

I tense a little at Olivia's name. "Will she be here tonight?" I ask, bracing myself.

He shakes his head. "No, prior engagement. That's why I have to make an appearance."

"Oh." I relax again, relieved. There's only so much stress I can take, and Caleb's presence is commanding enough of it right now. "Well, maybe this one won't be so bad. There's food, right?"

He smiles at me. "Yes, there'll be food."

We climb the main steps into the grand hall, and I catch glimpses of famous pieces of art as we're swallowed up by a crowd of impeccably dressed socialites.

If Caleb wasn't enthusiastic about the event, you could never tell. He works the crowd like a pro, introducing me to dozens of people, all of whom know him and greet him happily, like he's a member of their club. Then they run their eyes over me like I'm clearly *not*. I get the feeling they've seen Caleb with plenty of women before, and don't think they need to waste their time with me.

Luckily, the feeling's mutual, because I forget their names immediately. I hear an alphabet soup of titles—CEO, CFO, COO. But it all goes out in one ear and out the other. The only thing on my mind?

My date for the night.

I want him.

So much, I can't think straight. All I can focus on is his hand, warm on the curve of my back. The sound of his voice, seductive in my ear. The brush of his sleeve, reaching to shake yet another hand.

Bad girl. You'll be punished later.

The promise is driving me wild.

Whatever he has in mind, I'm itching for it, thirsting for it. And while I desperately want him to feel the same, he seems fine to keep me waiting, and all too happy to play this social game.

But appearances can be deceiving. He told me he hates these things.

And unruffled as he looks, maybe he's just as giddy with anticipation as I am.

"Gallagher!" Finally, Caleb greets someone with what sounds like genuine enthusiasm. It's a man around his age, with a shock of curly hair and a tan suit. They shake hands and slap each other on the back. "This is my buddy Jonathan," he introduces us. "I've known him since I was a kid."

"But don't expect me to tell any embarrassing stories," Jonathan greets me with a smile. "I'm bound by attorney-client privilege."

"You better be," Caleb chuckles. "The amount you bill."

"You have to pay for the best." Jonathan grins at me, the

first genuine smile I've received here all night. "Now, who's this lovely lady, and why haven't I heard about her before?"

"This is Juliet," Caleb replies—and doesn't elaborate.

I wish he would. At least then, I would have a clue how he sees me this evening. As his assistant? Date?

Conquest?

Jonathan doesn't seem to notice the vagueness of my introduction—or maybe he's used to Caleb showing up with a different woman every day of the week. "Lovely to meet you," he says. "And also, you have my sympathies, being dragged to a boring shindig like this. I hope Caleb makes it up to you later."

Caleb gives me a burning look. "I'm planning on it."

WE SIT DOWN TO DINNER, with a group of people discussing Aspen, and Palm Beach, and the merits of skiing versus sunshine at the holidays. Caleb gamely plays along, commenting on St Barts, and holding forth about lodge construction costs in Montana. I can't believe the ease with which he can play pretend, but maybe this is a side of his personality I just haven't seen before.

Then his hand sneaks under the tablecloth and finds my thigh.

He does it so effortlessly, without breaking his conversation with the old man across from him. They're discussing yachts. Apparently, Caleb's an expert yachtsman. I don't find this hard to believe because he's an expert at *everything*.

Especially the way he's touching me.

His hand brushes higher. On edge, I drop my butter knife and it clatters to the china plate.

Everyone turns to stare.

My hot face burns hotter. "Whoops!" I manage, and they all turn back to their gazpacho. An announcer begins a speech at the head of the room, distracting everyone. Caleb uses the cover to lean closer and whisper, "You're so tense."

"I wonder why?" I shoot back under my breath.

He chuckles. "I can think of a few ways to... Relax you."

His fingertips begin tracing tiny circles on the inside of my bare thigh.

I tense. "That would have the opposite effect," I remind him, and he smiles.

"Maybe so, but God, you'd look beautiful coming here, in front of everyone."

I try to keep my cool.

"I'm beginning to think you have an exhibitionist kink," I say coolly, sipping my water.

Caleb stifles a laugh. "What do you know about kink?" he murmurs in my ear, still caressing me out of sight, under the table.

Absolutely nothing I haven't read about in steamy fanfiction, but he doesn't have to know that.

"I know all kinds of things," I lie, tired of feeling like the wide-eyed innocent around all his sexual games.

"Interesting..." Caleb's fingers roam higher. "I can't wait to discover exactly what you know. And what I can teach you."

I inhale sharply. Right now, all I know is that I'm in serious danger of coming apart under his hands in the middle of a crowded ballroom. But luckily, before I can lose all composure, there's a thunderous round of applause—and everyone's looking in our direction.

I know Caleb is skilled, but a standing ovution?

"Congratulations," people at our table are saying.

I look at Caleb, confused. "I'll be right back," he says, getting to his feet. He strides swiftly to the podium and shakes the host's hand, accepting some kind of award.

That's when I notice the tasteful banner, and the printed

programs on our table. New York Society of the Arts honors our Donor of the Year: Caleb Sterling.

I gape. No wonder Caleb had to show up: He's the reason for the event!

"I'm not one for speeches," Caleb is saying into the mic. "But being honored like this is truly... Well, it's an honor. So many people work so hard on behalf of this organization, so, I'll dedicate this award to them. Thank you."

Applause erupts again as he leaves the podium. Making his way back to our table, people stop to congratulate him and offer words of praise. He accepts them politely, but I can tell, his impatience is growing. He's just about to rejoin me when an older guy intercepts him, red-faced and jovial.

"Sterling! Fine show, my friend." He stumbles a little, and holds onto a nearby chair for support. Clearly, that glass of champagne in his hand isn't his first tonight.

"Thank you," Caleb replies pleasantly.

"I only wish your old man was around to see it. You've done him proud, for sure."

Caleb's shoulders stiffen imperceptibly.

"He was a fine man, Jacob." The man sighs. "Damn shame, that accident. Damn shame."

Caleb doesn't answer, and the man moves off.

"Everything OK?" I ask, moving to his side.

"Fine." Caleb's voice is clipped, but he covers any emotion with a charming smile. "I've had enough of this place, that's all. Get your things, we're leaving. It's time for your punishment."

12

JULIET

THE RIDE back to Caleb's place is torturous. Caleb doesn't lay a hand on me, but somehow, it doesn't matter. Just knowing that he's seated there beside me is enough to drive my imagination wild. I don't know where he's taking me, or what he's planning for when we arrive. But based on every moment we've spent alone together in the past few days...

I'm in for the night of my life.

The car pulls up on an exclusive block, outside a sleek, modern building. Caleb sweeps me inside past the doorman, and uses a special key for the elevator.

Penthouse floor.

We ride up in silence, my anticipation thrumming in my veins. Caleb has barely said a word to me since we left the gala, and it's almost a relief not to have to manage polite small talk or casual conversation, when my body is wound tight like this.

Aching for release.

The doors slide open—directly into his apartment. Although, the word 'apartment' doesn't do the place justice.

"Wow," I breathe, stepping into the expanse of cool marble

and polished wood. He must have the entire floor, because the living area alone must be a thousand square feet, decorated with chic furniture, featuring sweeping views of the city out the floor-to-ceiling windows.

Caleb heads to the vast marble kitchen and browses his bar while I wander, taking it all in. Low, modern furniture, sleek tech, minimal art… It's gorgeous, but as I look closer, I realize it's just like his office at work: strangely impersonal.

Anyone could live here. Anyone outrageously wealthy, that is.

If I'd hoped that his living space might offer me more insight into the man that is Caleb Sterling, I'm disappointed. He's as much of an enigma as ever.

Music sounds, low jazz, drifting from the invisible built-in speakers. Caleb strolls to join me in the living room. He hands me a drink, and I take a gulp, my anticipation tangling up with nerves until I can't think of what to say.

"You don't have to be nervous," Caleb murmurs, clearly seeing my jitters. He reaches out and runs a hand down the side of my cheek, stroking softly. "You won't do anything you don't want to do."

"Oh." I exhale. "OK."

He gives me a crooked smile. "In fact, you'll be begging for it."

"You seem pretty sure of yourself," I retort, trying to sound more confident than I feel. Because standing in the middle of a billionaire's penthouse in a diamond necklace and gown?

Not my usual date-night plans.

But my pretense at playing it cool lasts all of five seconds, until the moment Caleb pulls me closer, and kisses me.

Hot and possessive, tantalizingly sensual. I melt to his touch immediately, sinking into his arms, opening my mouth to him, inviting the slick invasion of his tongue.

God, this man can kiss.

But it's not all he can do. His hands roam over my body, and I feel the heat of him burning through our clothes.

He steps back abruptly.

"Stand over there," he tells me, nodding to a spot in the middle of the room.

Heart in my throat, I do as he says.

Caleb sinks into a leather chair, and sits back, watching me with dark, glittering eyes.

"Red." He says.

"Excuse me?"

"That's your safe word. If you want me to stop, at any time, just say 'red'."

I exhale. *A safe word*? My sexual experience to date has never included anything like this. Not even close. But the idea that I still have some control over this whole thing is reassuring. That even though Caleb has me dizzy with desire, I hold the final trump card.

I give a nod.

"Good." Caleb gives me a slow, molten smile. "Now strip for me."

I gulp.

"Here?"

Caleb doesn't take his eyes off me. "I won't tell you again."

A shiver rolls through me at the sudden steel in his voice. It's the voice he uses to scold people in the office, inherently commanding.

And utterly undeniable.

And just like that, a part of me relaxes.

He's the one in control here. I don't need to make a decision, or wonder how to act: Trying to be seductive, or second-guess how I'm *supposed* to behave.

All I need to do is exactly what he tells me.

Obey.

I'm shocked by the erotic thrill that sparks through me. I've never done anything like this before, but if I'm honest...

I've always wondered. Dreamed about it.

Fantasized.

A firm hand. A sharp word. The sting of a palm against my ass. Those are the images that chase me when I'm alone at night, fingers reaching between my thighs, and now... ?

Now I get to explore them, for real.

I take a deep breath, wetting my lips. Then I reach behind me, and slowly unzip the dress.

Caleb relaxes back in his chair.

His eyes are on me, watching. The lights are dim. And the music keeps playing, a sultry refrain that seems to seep into my bloodstream, making my hips sway in time to the beat.

I feel sexy. *Desirable.*

I slide the dress over my shoulders, revealing my strapless lace bra.

Caleb takes a drink.

I peel the dress lower, shimmying it down over my bare stomach. It falls to the ground, and I step free, standing there in my lingerie and heels. And the necklace.

On display.

My pulse skitters. I hold my breath, waiting for his next words.

"More."

Caleb's voice is rough, and I shudder at the foreign rasp.

Slowly, I unsnap my bra, and let it fall. The air is cool against my bare breasts, and I feel my nipples pucker at the chill.

He sits forward in his seat.

"More," he says it again, demanding. It wouldn't occur to me to disobey.

In a trance, I peel my panties down. Now I'm naked, there in the middle of the room, wearing nothing but the diamond choker. His eyes on me. *Devouring.*

His jaw is tense. He grips the whiskey glass.

I did this.

"Show me." he growls. "Show me everything."

I straighten my posture, my heart racing in my chest. Slowly, I turn for him, presenting every inch of my body for his inspection. My skin crackles with awareness. It's like I can feel his gaze on my body, the slow molten path of his eyes spreading heat across every inch of me. I clench, already aching for him. When I finally face him again, the pure lust in his expression takes my breath away.

He wants me.

He *needs* me.

Caleb beckons, and I move immediately to him. My whole body is tingling, crying out for his touch. But it won't be eased just yet, because with one brief order, he tells me exactly what he wants to happen know.

"Get on your knees. Hands behind your back."

I feel a rush as I follow his instructions. The carpet is thick beneath my bare knees, and I move into position between his legs. "Time to finish what you started."

He unzips his pants, and frees his cock for me, guiding it towards my mouth.

I lick his shaft, then open wide for him, and I'm rewarded with a groan as I take him deep between my lips.

Damn.

It's like a drug, the desire coursing through me, hot in my veins. Driving me on as I lick and tease him, giddy with adrenaline. Caleb knots my hair in his hands, controlling my pace exactly the way he likes it. He tugs firmly on my hair, moving me how he wants, and I obey him without question, thrilled at his dominance.

The world contracts to just the feel of his cock in my mouth, pumping faster, velvet on steel. I'm so turned on, I can't think straight. My nipples are stiff, aching. I'm wet, trembling, and he hasn't even touched me yet.

I look up, locking eyes with him, hoping I'm doing this right.

"Yes," he hisses. "Just like that."

There's something animal, primitive in the way he's looking at me that fills me with a new fire. I flick my tongue over the head of his cock, teasing, and Caleb lets out another ragged groan.

He grips my head tighter, thrusting into my mouth now, so deep he hits the back of my throat. I almost gag at the size of him, gasping for air, but it's thrilling, too. To be overwhelmed like this.

Used as he sees fit.

I feel another shudder of lust. His breathing deepens. He's close. I suck harder at his beautiful cock, trying to take the thick length deeper into my throat as his fingers tighten in my hair, almost painful.

But just pleasurable enough.

I feel his thighs tense underneath me, the telltale leap of his cock between my lips. I start to pull away, but his hand remains, heavy there on the back of my head.

"No," he says, half an order, and half a desperate groan. "Take it all. Be a good girl, and swallow every last drop."

Oh God.

I feel a damp rush of desire between my thighs at the command. It's so dirty.

So raw.

So unbelievably hot.

I moan around his cock, taking him deeper still. His fingers grip me, hard, and then he erupts with an animal growl, unleashing a hot jet of cum down my throat.

I take it all, just the way he told me to.

Every last drop.

When he's finally done, he slowly zips up his pants and pulls me off him. "Good girl," he purrs, looking down at me with satisfaction, and I feel a rush of pride.

He reaches out, and cups my cheek, stroking softly. "Look at you," he murmurs, lips spreading in a smug smile. "You're trembling. You liked it."

I flush. "Yes," I admit, shame and delight mingling in my blood. It's intoxicating, discovering just how far I'll go for this man.

Just how much I like it.

Caleb's hand trails lower, to my bare breast. He toys with my nipple for a moment, and I let out a moan, desperate for his touch.

For some kind of release.

I'm wound so tight, so turned on I think I might explode, but all Caleb does is pinch one stiff nipple before releasing me again.

"Please..." I find myself gasping, missing the caress.

He arches an eyebrow.

"I need..." I try again, but I can't bring myself to say the words.

Caleb smiles. "I know exactly what you need, sweet girl," he coos, his voice seductive. His eyes flashing with wicked intention. "And I'm going to give it to you. But first... First, you need to be taught a lesson."

Swiftly, he scoops me up, and carries me over to the low coffee table. He places me down on it, on my hands and knees.

"Your little stunt in the car the other day..." he says, pacing slowly around me. The concrete is hard and cold against my skin, and the position is unnatural, *exposed*, but I don't dare move.

I don't dare *breathe.*

"You almost distracted me on a work call," he continues, his voice thrillingly harsh. He trails a hand lightly over my naked back. Possessively. "You tried to make a fool of me. You tried to show me who's boss."

I shift, my heart racing. My head is facing down, the diamond choker heavy at my neck. I can't see what he's doing, I can only see his footsteps circle the coffee table, and feel the soft caress of his hand, coming to a stop on the curve of my bare ass.

Caleb pauses, and leans over to whisper in my ear. "There's only one person in charge here, Juliet. And it will always be me, do you understand?"

He squeezes my ass, possessive.

I gasp.

"Do you understand?"

"Yes!" I blurt, clutching hold of the edge of the table to keep my balance. "I'm sorry. I won't do it again."

"No. You won't."

Suddenly, he spanks me.

Hard.

I let out a shriek of surprise—and pain. My flesh stings from the impact.

"Count to ten," Caleb instructs me. "Do it now."

He spanks me again, and I jolt forwards with the force of the impact. "O... One," I manage, gasping for air.

"Good girl."

His hand hits my ass again, harder this time, and I let out a noise of pain. But then, just as fast, his hand is stroking me. Soothing the fire. Caressing softly, easing the sting.

"Two," I blurt, feeling my heat return. The low ache of need, right there between my thighs.

The third time, his hand strays lower, fingers skimming over my pussy.

I gasp, leaning back into his hand. But then the touch is gone.

The fourth blow hits my other ass cheek, the sound echoing in the empty apartment. I'm so wet, he can probably see it by now.

Smell it on me.

But I don't care.

"I like you like this," he muses, circling me again. "On your knees, so obedient. My handprints all over your sweet ass."

I moan in answer, shaking. I don't know how long I can stay this way, but I do know one thing:

I'm not moving until he tells me to.

Caleb strokes my back again, fingertips roaming down between my thighs. I moan again, pressing eagerly against his hand as his strokes over my clit, and then slowly thrusts two fingers inside me.

I hear a chuckle. "So wet," he says approvingly. "It looks like you enjoy my punishment."

God yes.

He flexes his fingers deeper, and I grip the table, pressing back against him, trying to take them as deep as I can. "God yes, like that," Caleb instructs me, his voice thick. "Fuck yourself on my fingers. Get yourself off."

I do as he says.

I know it's shameful, to be displayed like this. Naked on my hands and knees, mindlessly grinding back against this man's fingers, chasing any release I can find, but I'm too far gone to care. Over and over, I thrust back on him, as Caleb pumps deeper inside me with one hand, the other still stroking over my shoulders... My back... My ass. Over me, and...

In between.

I freeze as he skims down, down the crevice between my cheeks. I hear his chuckle. "An innocent, are we?"

I feel a nudge, a brush of foreign touch circling me, *there*.

I gasp, clenching in surprise around his fingers.

Caleb flexes, and *fuck*, he rubs something on my inner wall, something that makes me see stars.

"That's right, sweetheart," Caleb says, sounding amused. "You don't even know what your body is capable of, not yet. But I'm going to show you. I'm going to show you a pleasure you never dreamed was possible."

He rubs again, a dizzying rhythm, and I feel the heat rise, faster. Quicksilver in my veins.

"Oh God," I cry, panting. Chasing the pleasure. Thrusting back against his hands. "Caleb... Caleb please!"

"You're forgetting something, my sweet," he says, pausing. I want to sob. No, he can't stop!

"I haven't finished punishing you yet."

His spanking takes me by surprise: Hard and sharp, pain bursting through the pleasure. I cry out, tears welling in the corner of my eyes. But his fingers are still inside me, milking that special spot, as he alternates a punishing slap with a deep, full thrust of his fingers.

"Five. Six. Seven."

I'm howling, but with pleasure or pain, I can't even tell any more. I just need this. More. *More*.

"Eight. Nine."

I feel the pleasure cresting. Fuck. *Fuck. Right there*.

"Ten."

He lands a final blow and it's enough to send me hurtling over the edge. I come apart with a scream, shattering with a rush of pure ecstasy so sharp, I swear I almost black out. I fall forwards on the table as it surges through me, waves rolling over and over, consuming me, unravelling me, until I'm left collapsed there, dizzy and utterly spent.

Oh.

My.

God.

I lay there, reeling. I didn't know an orgasm could be like that. Hell, I didn't know *sex* could be like that.

"Hey."

I look over. Caleb has crouched beside the table, his face just inches from mine. "Are you alive, or... ?" He reaches out, and gently brushes a lock of sweaty hair from my face.

The tenderness of the gesture takes me by surprise.

I sit up. "Or, have you killed me with pleasure?" I ask, finishing his question. He smirks, but I can't hold it against him.

That was, hands down, the most intense sexual experience of my life.

I gingerly stretch. "I'm alive," I confirm. "Just about."

"Good." Caleb helps me to my feet, and gives me a smoldering look that just about takes my breath away all over again. "Because I'm not done with you yet."

I can't begin to imagine what else is in store, but as he's leading me towards what I'm hoping is the bedroom, the sound of a ringtone comes.

Caleb pauses.

"You're off the clock, remember?" I tell him, teasing, but it's like the shutters have already come down. He strides over to a cabinet by the door and pulls a cellphone from the drawer.

"Yes?" he asks sharply. "Fine. I understand."

He hangs up. "I'm afraid you need to leave now," he says, all business again. He buttons his shirt, and adjusts his belt.

I blink at him in disbelief.

"Are you serious?"

I'm standing buck naked in a million-dollar necklace. The man has just spanked me and given me an epic orgasm all at the same time, which is multitasking I would be impressed by, if he wasn't suddenly kicking me out the door.

"I'll call a car for you." Caleb says blandly. "Get home safe."

And then with that oh-so-romantic parting comment, he walks into the elevator, and the doors shut behind him.

He's gone.

I can't believe it. What the hell just happened? I feel a rush of rejection, and humiliation, and a dozen other awful feelings.

I scramble for my dress and pull it on. I don't want to stay here a minute longer now that I've been so unceremoniously kicked to the curb.

It's only when I'm on my way out that I realize: The phone he answered? It wasn't his usual work phone.

It must be the one he keeps for shady, secret business. The kind of business that pulls him away from a naked, willing woman at midnight without a backwards glance.

Whatever the hell is going on with Caleb Sterling, it can't be good.

13

JULIET

THE WEEKEND IS MISERABLE.

I pinball from shame, to anger, to lust, to humiliation and back to pure rage again.

I can't stop thinking about Caleb. He treats me to a lavish evening, gives me the most amazing sexual experience of my life and then...

Walks out on me.

What kind of asshole does that?

The kind of handsome, sexy billionaire asshole who dates a new woman every week, I remind myself. Caleb probably has his routine down cold. Why would I be any different?

I have a wounded ego. Not to mention a sore backside. Every time I sit down, the slight sting reminds me of him.

And just how good it felt to obey him, on my hands and knees. Begging for more.

Which is exactly how Caleb said he liked his women.

How does that saying go? When someone shows you who they are, believe them.

Well, Caleb gave me plenty of warning. He made his filthy intentions clear. I guess I just thought it would go differently.

To bed, instead of home, alone, in his swanky car.

I'M STILL WALLOWING on my bed Sunday afternoon when Kelsey pokes her head around the door.

"Really?" she asks, sounding sympathetic. "You know you've been moping around all weekend."

"Your point?" I call back, but it's muffled by a pillow.

"Come on. Have some dinner. I picked up pizza... You need the calories, if you're going to wallow much harder."

I sigh.

But she's right. I need to get up. I'm going to have to go to work tomorrow anyway, so I can't simply lie in bed forever, hoping the world—and a certain unfeeling billionaire—goes away.

Rolling out of bed, I go to the kitchen, where she's setting out the greasy pizza box and a couple of paper napkins. I join her on one of the counter stools, but I'm not hungry.

For pizza, anyway.

"I feel like an idiot," I sigh. "Maybe this is his big routine: Hook us, then keep us dangling."

"Are you sure it wasn't an emergency?" Kelsey asks. I filled her in on the details. Well, most of them.

"He didn't say anything about an emergency. He didn't say anything at all. Just walked out the door. While I was naked!"

"Well, he is an important guy. Places to go, people to see. And..." Her eyes land on the necklace on the end of the counter. She snatches it up. "Whoa. What is this?"

"The necklace he had me wear."

"Real diamonds?" Kelsey's eyes bug out of her head. "This has got to be worth…"

"A million bucks, at least."

She drops it like a hot coal. "And you just left it sitting on our kitchen counter?"

"I don't know what else to do with it. I guess I'll give it back to him tomorrow at work. Or leave it on his desk so I don't have to look him in the eye."

"Wow." Kelsey shakes her head. "Your life is way more interesting than it was last week."

And she doesn't know the half of it.

"What if he calls?" she asks, cocking her head. "Will you go out with him again?"

"Nope." I grit my teeth, determined. "He had his chance. If he has better things to do than ravish me while I'm literally right there in front of him, then let him. I'm not getting involved again."

"Reeeaaallly?" Kelsey doesn't look convinced.

"Really." I insist. "I do have some pride left. And self-respect."

"Good for you. Stay strong," she cheers, shoveling the rest of her pizza into her mouth. "Look, I have to go to the salon for a wedding updo, but when I get back, you and I should go out."

I sigh and look down at myself. Old sweatpants. Even older robe. I look like crud. I feel worse. "I don't know."

"I'm not taking no for an answer! You need to move on, leave the bastard billionaire behind." She grabs her stuff. "Take a shower! I'll be back by six."

She's right. I need to leave him behind.

When she's gone, I go into the bathroom and turn the water on. Slipping out of my robe, I catch a glimpse of my ass in the mirror.

Mottled red. *Marked by him.*

I rub lightly at it, wishing it away. Not that that helps. Bastard.

Kelsey's right. I need to leave him behind.

I take a long shower, trying to scrub away the desire still prickling beneath my skin. I'm just toweling off, when there's a knock at the door.

I freeze.

What if it's Caleb?

My heart races as I edge closer. Should I let him in? What could he want? Should I—

I peek through the peephole. And my heart comes back down to earth with a thump.

It's Olivia.

Suddenly, reality comes crashing back in.

I've been so swept up in desire, consumed with Caleb and our crazy sexual connection that I've forgotten why I'm at Sterling Cross in the first place.

My secret assignment: Catching Caleb in the act.

I quickly collect myself and open the door. "Hi, Olivia! I didn't expect you."

"Sorry to drop by like this," she says, giving me a smile. "How are things? Can you talk?"

"Sure." I stand aside and invite her in. "Sorry about the mess," I add quickly, knowing this place is nothing compared to her spotless mansion.

"Are you kidding? It's so cute. Eclectic." Olivia flashes another smile. "I heard you made an appearance with Caleb at the museum event. How ever did you manage that?"

I gulp. "He was the one who suggested it. I was working late, I'm sure I was just the nearest warm body around."

"Yes, well... Anything that gets you closer to the truth." Olivia's smile looks a little more pinched, but she quickly continues, "Have you been able to get a look at his phone yet?"

"Yes, but there was nothing on it. I think he has two of them."

Olivia frowns. "Two phones? That's weird."

"Not necessarily." For some reason, I find myself defending him. "Some guys keep two phones, you know, for dates. Personal and business."

"Well, Caleb certainly gets around." Olivia gives a sharp laugh.

I feel a burn of humiliation. He certainly got his way around my body the other night.

"Anything else suspicious?" Olivia presses. "Acting strangely? Mysterious appointments?"

"No, except..." I stop.

"Except what?"

I pause. How do I say this? "He did rush off after the gala," I tell her carefully. "It was odd. He got a call and just took off."

"I heard you left quite early," Olivia says.

"We did." I burn. "This was... After. On the way to his place," I add, fudging the details just enough to save my virtue.

"Oh." Olivia's eyes widen.

There's silence. I wonder what she thinks of me. She told me to get close to him, but I don't think she figured on this close. What if she's mad?

But after a moment, Olivia seems to collect herself. She gives me a smile. "Look, Juliet, I'm not judging you. Caleb is a very charming man, and Lord knows, he can be very... Persuasive. But you should know, he's an expert at acting the part. He plays the part of the dutiful CEO to our investors. A generous philanthropist. He's always playing a part. To the press, to his employees... To his women."

"Oh." I deflate, remembering again how Caleb turned on the charm at the gala, even when it didn't mean anything to him.

Is that what he's been doing with me?

Olivia seems to take pity on me. She comes over and puts her arm around me. "Oh, Juliet. You didn't believe his lines, did you? You're a beautiful woman, sitting right outside his door all day. And Caleb, well, he's like most man. He values convenience. It's no wonder he's turned his attention on you."

My mouth opens, but nothing comes out. My cheeks heat.

Olivia shakes her head sadly. "I've known him for a long time. He seduces just about every woman he comes across. *He's incorrigible that way.* Showers you with attention, expensive gifts, flowers, the whole nine yards. Then, when he gets what he wants... Game over. He can't get away from them fast enough."

A sick feeling swirls in my gut. Is he going to throw me away? Has he already?

"Which would make things tricky for us, don't you think?" Olivia continues.

Us. The plan. Right.

"So what should I do?" I ask, head spinning.

"Don't let him add you to his list of conquests," Olivia advises. "As long as he's chasing you, you still have value. Which means, you still have a job, and access to the proof. Otherwise... Well, if you can't get near Caleb, you can't really be much help to me, can you?"

The question dangles there. A faint threat.

Now my sickness is full-on nausea. I have to swallow back the bile in my throat. If I don't get the info... I can't get the reward—and help my mom.

I nod, trying to keep my composure. "Thanks for the info. I'll keep that in mind."

"Good. Thanks Juliet. You're doing great. Just—keep the pressure on."

I see Olivia out, but as she's stepping into the hallway, she crosses with a delivery guy just coming up the stairs. His arms are full of a massive bouquet of roses.

Olivia lets out a sharp laugh. "See? Right on time. From the company account at Le Rouge, no doubt."

She swans off, and I accept the delivery and head back inside. The roses are gorgeous, but there's a card perched on top. From Le Rouge florist, just like Olivia said.

J- Sorry about last night. We will pick up where we left off. – C

Oh, will we?

Anger rises, hot in my veins. He may be sexy as hell, but he's also a shady, unfeeling asshole.

And I've had enough of being his plaything.

AN HOUR LATER, I'm at a local bar with Kelsey, drinking Caleb right off my mind. Not that there's enough tequila in the world to make me forget his commanding blue eyes... Or that delicious dominating voice.

"So, he sends you flowers, he calls you numerous times and you do... What, again?" Kelsey asks.

"Nothing," I snap, shoving my phone into my bag.

Three texts from Caleb, each one telling me to call him, getting increasingly more demanding.

She gives me a look. "But it's *Caleb Sterling.*"

"I don't care if it's God. I can't do this. I have to work with him."

She runs a fingertip over the rim of her margarita and licks the salt off. "You have more willpower than most women in the city, girl. I guarantee it'd take a lot less for them to drop their panties."

My willpower is not nearly as impressive as she thinks. I

shift on my stool and scan the bar, desperate for something to help get Caleb Sterling out of my head. This is my second margarita, and so far, all it's done is make me want him more.

"Distract me," I tell her. Kelsey sees something behind me and smirks.

"I have just the thing."

I turn—and a guy strolling over to us. He's the polar opposite of Caleb: Hot, in that rough-around-the-edges way, with stubble on his jaw and tattoos peeking out from under the sleeves of his vintage Rolling Stones T-shirt.

Still... It's not Caleb.

"Don't look now, but a major babe is on his way," Kelsey says under her breath.

As much as I want to be in the mood to flirt, I'm not. "He's all yours."

"Sorry," she says, grabbing her purse and shoving off the stool. "I've got to go to the ladies'."

Great. Abandoned. I groan as he approaches.

"Hi there," he says, flashing me a charming grin. "Can I get you another drink?"

I don't look at him. "I don't think so. I'll be throwing up in the parking lot."

He laughs. "That's because you're drinking all that sugar. You need a real drink. Two whiskeys," he says, already ordering from the bartender.

"Really, I'm fine."

"Then more for me." He smiles.

"I'm Logan," he says, extending a hand.

I force myself to shake it. "Juliet."

He studies me a moment, then snaps his fingers. "I've seen you before."

I shrug. "I come here with my roommate sometimes."

"No, not here... Midtown. Earlier this week. A coffee shop there."

"Oh. I just started a new job in that area," I explain.

"I knew it." Logan grins. "I always remember a pretty face."

I roll my eyes.

"Too much?" he laughs. "It's the God's honest truth. So how's the new job going?"

"Fine," I lie.

"Ouch. That bad?"

"No... I just... My boss is a lot to handle, that's all," I find myself confiding. Logan's drinks arrive, and he takes a sip, looking open and curious and *not* Caleb Sterling.

"You have my sympathies. Those CEO billionaires are all the same. So, what does the bastard have you doing?"

I pause. Since when did I mention my boss was a CEO billionaire?

In fact... In a city of millions, what are the odds this guy sees me getting coffee then shows up here when I'm out for a drink?

I get down from my stool. "I have to go," I say.

"So soon?" Logan looks disappointed. "Why don't I get your number? I'd love to take you to dinner sometime."

"No thanks."

I hightail it away from him and grab Kelsey. "We need to go."

"Already?" she looks behind me. "What was that all about?"

"I don't know. That guy was a little intense. Asking questions about my job..."

"Really? But he was so hot!"

I shuttle her toward the doors. "He was, but that doesn't mean he can't be a stalker."

When we get back to the apartment, I find Caleb's town car parked at the curb.

My heart drops.

But he's not there. It's just his driver waiting—for me. "Caleb Sterling wants to meet you for dinner. I'm under instructions to bring you there."

Kelsey grins. "Ooh, fancy."

"Not fancy," I correct her, annoyed. "Presumptuous." I turn to him. "Tell Caleb Sterling thanks, but no thanks. I'll be staying home tonight."

I march inside, fuming.

So he sends his driver to fetch me? He's too important to take the time out of his day to come see me on his own? And he expects me to drop everything and rush to his side at a moment's notice?

I don't think so.

That will show him I'm not so easy to boss around. And that he can't buy my forgiveness with a bunch of roses—like all the other girls.

My pride lasts as long as it takes for my phone to light up with a text.

You know you're thinking about me.

I want to tell him I'm not. But he knows when I'm lying, even better than I do.

I make a noise of frustration and head to bed.

My phone lights up again.

Do you know all the things I could be doing to you right now?

I bury a muffled cry in my pillow. No, I don't know; but I can imagine. Images flash through my mind, hot and sensual, dirty and wild.

Just the way he planned.

But Caleb doesn't have to know what he's doing to me. I

make a promise, that no matter what, I won't be fooled by him again.

I'll be strong. I'll resist temptation.

And I'll help Olivia find the evidence to get him out of my life for good.

14

JULIET

BY THE TIME Monday rolls around, I'm more determined than ever that my erotic night with Caleb was a mistake. A delicious, mind-blowing, orgasmic mistake, but a mistake nonetheless.

And it absolutely can't happen again.

Still, I know that Caleb isn't the type of man to give up so easily, so I'm not surprised when he calls me into his office as soon as I arrive at work.

Squaring my shoulders, I walk in. "You wanted to see me?"

Caleb's at his desk with a pile of paperwork, but he sets it aside when I walk in. "Juliet. Good. I need to apologize for leaving so abruptly the other night."

"No problem." I manage a casual shrug. "These things happen."

"You're not mad at me?" He seems surprised.

"Not at all." My tone is cool. "Oh, that reminds me."

I reach into the pocket of my sweater, pull out the necklace, and set it on his desk. "Thanks for loaning it," I say casually.

"You should keep it." Caleb smiles. "Wear it to dinner with me tonight."

"No thank you."

He blinks. "You have plans? Break them."

"No." I meet his eyes. *Stay strong.* "I'm not going to dinner with you. In fact, I won't see you outside the office again. Friday was... A mistake. Going forward, I'd like to keep things professional. I'm sure you understand."

If he's disappointed by that, he doesn't show a ripple. "Of course." His eyes snake down my body. "So you've recovered?"

His gaze is locked on my ass. So, that's his way of being professional? "Absolutely. It isn't even a memory."

I turn to leave. He says, "So let me know when you'd like to pick up where we left off."

I stop and level my most unaffected gaze at him. "Believe it or not, *I* don't want to. This... *Thing* between us is not of interest to me anymore."

"Is that so?" Caleb smirks.

He's not buying it. And for good reason. I've never told a bigger lie in all my life.

Somehow, I manage to nod. "Yes. Will that be all, Mr. Sterling?"

"For now." He's still smirking, like my determination is amusing to him. Like it's *funny* that I've just told him to go screw himself.

My scowl deepens. "I'll be at my desk if you need me."

I manage a step before he says, "Juliet?"

I freeze but don't turn this time. I've had just about enough of this. I'm going to hide out in another department so he won't bother me—

"Victoria called in sick today. So you'll need to make yourself available to me."

I grimace. *Make yourself available to me.* I plaster a bland smile on my face. "Whatever you say."

I stalk back to my desk, preparing for war. Hardening myself for the torture. Thankfully, though, he doesn't toy with me like I thought he would. Sure, every time he leaves his office, I feel his eyes on me, and it's like walking on eggshells. But by the end of the day, he's simply sending me curt, professional emails. At first, I'm happy.

Then I realize that if all I do is interact with him via email, I'm never going to have any opportunities to get a closer look at his schedule.

Or look for that second burner phone.

"You look kind of flushed," Mara remarks, dropping by my desk with a folder of proofs for Caleb to review, and a box of donuts. "Are you feeling OK?"

"Oh, yes," I say, deleting another one-word email from him, thanking me for sending over a sales report. "It's just been crazy, with Victoria out."

She winces. "Bad timing. With Sterling being in such a grumpy mood. He's been on a tear today."

"Has he?"

She nods and checks the clock on the wall. "Thank goodness it's almost quitting time. Any big plans?"

I laugh. "If a hot bath and *Bachelor* marathon count."

"Ooh, you're watching too?" she lights up. "I'm driving my boyfriend crazy, he doesn't understand. But did you see last week's episode?"

We trade gossip for a while, and find we have a ton of interests in common. "You'll have to come over one night and watch with me," Mara insists. "It'll be fun."

"Maybe next week?" I suggest, pleased to be making a friend. And that there's someone in this building who doesn't hate me, or want to fuck me.

We wish each other a good night and I start to put my things together. Then Caleb emerges from his office. I brace myself for his charm offensive: Dirty talk, or flirtation, trying to make me regret my choice.

But then he just stalks out, briefcase in hand, without so much a look at me. "Good night, Juliet."

I just stare after him. I've survived. But I can't help feeling a twinge of regret.

Has he really given up so easily?

But when I get home, I find he hasn't quit just yet. Another gorgeous bouquet is waiting for me, this time a stunning display of hydrangeas in purples and blue.

I check the card. It's from Caleb.

It's still of interest to me. Tell me what I have to do. – C

I stare at it, feeling the cracks forming in my façade.

No. He left you alone, Juliet. Don't forget that.

I crumple the note and contemplate tossing the flowers in the dumpster. In the end, I only bring them inside because they smell nice, and well... I like flowers.

That's the only reason. I swear.

BY THE END of the week, he's sent me three more bouquets of increasing size and opulence. Candy. Expensive chocolates. A gift basket full of luxurious L'Occitane bath products and La Mer skincare.

I tell myself he's got a personal shopper picking them out. Hell, he probably keeps a supply in stock. But still...

The cracks in my façade are growing wider. It's always the same. He's uber-professional in the office, just like I asked him to be. And then he sends me these gifts.

"I'm telling you," Kelsey remarks, eyeing the latest delivery.

"This isn't just hookup material. Maybe this guy really has feelings for you."

"Caleb doesn't get *feelings*." I snap back. "Like Olivia said, he's flighty. I might be his latest obsession, but once he gets done with me, he'll move on."

Not that knowing that is making it any easier to resist him.

On Friday, Victoria's still out sick. Which means I have even more work to keep track of. But when I power up my computer, I see a new email in my personal account.

From Meadow View residential home.

Dear Ms. Nichols: Your account is past due.

I read the rest of it with growing horror. Yes, I've been delinquent on payments. I worked out a plan, spreading them out as far as I could, but apparently, not far enough.

If the bill is not paid in full by June 16th, we will have to start eviction proceedings, and you will forfeit the place to another patient on the wait-list.

June sixteenth. Meaning, three days from now.

My heart drops.

Eviction? I never thought it would get this far, this soon. Where could my mom go? She needs round-the-clock care, and besides that, she can't deal with change. Her routine is the only thing that keeps her calm; the nurses it's taken a year to warm up to, the garden where she likes to sit.

I can't take that away from her. It's all she has left.

I open my checking account and find the equivalent of a week's worth of rent. Panic surges through my body when I look up and see Caleb, heading my way.

He sets a coffee on the edge of my desk. "Iced mocha latte. For you."

I can't be flattered that he remembered my drink order.

I don't need anyone being charming around me. Not now.

No, my stomach is churning with dread and I'm about to lose my composure.

"It's Friday." Caleb continues, lounging there. He shoots me a smoldering look. "Any fun plans for the weekend?"

Fun? I stare at him in disbelief. Like I can even think about having fun when everything I've worked so hard to keep together is crumbling before my very eyes.

"I was thinking of taking a little trip. I have a place outside the city," he adds. "You should come. And *come.*"

I shake my head. I've had enough. I can't do this anymore. "Stop. Just stop. All of it," I cry, tears pricking the corners of my eyes. "This hot and cold act. Playing professional one minute and trying to seduce me the next. It's always on your terms. Everything *you* want. Well, I'm done with it!" I explode, scrambling to my feet. "Now you need to back off!"

For the first time, there's something like surprise on Caleb Sterling's perfect face. But I don't stick around to see it. Humiliation flushes through me, hot and full of regret. I push back my chair, and flee.

I manage to find an empty stairwell in the back of the building, with nobody inside. I sink down on a cold concrete step, and dial Meadow View with shaking hands.

"Hi, Mr. Castle? This is Juliet Nichols. I'm calling about an email I received?"

"Yes, Ms. Nichols. How can I help?"

"Well, I'm having an issue with the payment," I admit, crossing my fingers that I can buy just a little more time. "I should be coming into more money shortly, but it hasn't yet hit my account. Is there a way I can file another extension? It'll be just one more, I promise."

There was a pause. "I'm sorry, Ms. Nichols, but we've already given you as much time as we can.

I swallow hard. I can't pull my mother from the home. The

last place was a nightmare—dark, damp, with cramped rooms. My mother never looked clean. I imagine her, back in that place, and tears spring to my eyes. "So you're just going to kick her out?"

"Unless the account is settled, I'm sorry. We have no choice. She'll have to find someplace else to live."

I hang up, feeling utterly despairing.

There's nothing I can do. I've failed her, when she needs me the most.

"What's going on?"

My head snaps up. Caleb is standing in the landing above me. And he heard everything.

I quickly wipe the tears from my eyes. "Nothing."

I get up, and try to hurry past him, but he blocks my path. "Juliet. You're crying. Look, if this is about us—"

"Not everything's about you!" I explode again.

He raises his hands. "Woah, it's OK. Just tell me what's wrong and I'll fix it."

"You can't." I shake my head. "It's my mother's nursing home. They're kicking her out."

He frowns. "What facility is it?"

"Meadow View, out in Queens," I reply. He whips out his phone. "What are you doing?" I ask, my anxiety rising.

Caleb taps at the screen, then puts it to his ear.

"Caleb," I try, confused, but he just holds up a finger to me. "Yes, I need to speak with someone about a patient, by the name of Nichols."

Dread sweeps through me. What is he doing?

Caleb begins heading back upstairs, talking in a low voice. I hurry to try and catch up.

"Mmmhmm... I understand... Yes, that won't be necessary. I will be paying the outstanding bill in full. And in future, please direct all financial matters to my attention. I'll be taking care of them from now on."

Caleb hangs up, and turns to me. "The problem has been taken care of." Then he saunters back to his office.

I stop dead in the hallway in disbelief.

What the hell?

I charge after him, and burst through his office doors. "What was that?" I demand. "You think you can just buy me?"

He gives me an even look. "I'm not buying anything. You had a problem, I have the resources to fix it. So I did."

"But..." I'm speechless. "That place isn't cheap. She'll need to stay there for years. Decades, maybe."

"I understand." Caleb looks at me with sympathy in his eyes. "You didn't tell me, about her condition."

"Because it's none of your business."

But my voice falters. He's really just paid our bill in full —*forever*?

I've heard a lot of things about Caleb Sterling in the past. He's a thief. He's blessed in bed. He has an insatiable appetite for women. People have called him hot, egocentric, hard-headed... But no one has ever called him generous.

He takes a step towards me, "Juliet. I know I've been... Distant. Careless, even. But I'm not the man you think I am." His voice is quiet. Sincere. "Give me another chance."

"See. You did do this just to buy me," I say in disgust.

"No." Caleb insists. "If you want to keep things just professional between us, then I swear I won't ask you again. But you feel it too, this connection. I know you do."

His eyes blaze into mine, and I can't deny the rush I feel, just being so close. It's instinct.

It's inevitable.

I part my lips, and the word tumbles out.

"Yes."

15

JULIET

IF I HAD any second thoughts about giving Caleb his second chance, they melt away the next morning, when he picks me up to whisk me out to the Hamptons for the day.

"Your chariot awaits," he says, holding open the door to the convertible Mercedes. I'm not a car person, but even I can tell this is a gorgeous model. But not as gorgeous as the man sliding behind the wheel.

"You look... Different," I say, studying him as we hit the road. It's not just his casual outfit: a linen shirt, open at his throat, and dark wash jeans. He seems more relaxed than I've seen before. Lighter.

"A beautiful day with a beautiful woman," Caleb says, flashing me a grin from behind his Ray-Ban Wayfarer shades. "What's not to like?"

I smile back. I still can't believe that he solved all my problems with one call—and a very large check—and I can't deny that it's a weight off my mind, too.

Plus, a little voice whispers, reminding me that now my

mom's living situation is secured, I don't need Olivia's payoff anymore.

I try to push that thought away, but as we're pulling onto the highway, his phone rings.

I wonder, which phone is it?

The incoming call flashes up on the car system, and I brace myself for Caleb to flip the switch again: into work-mode CEO, or shady and detached. But instead, he clicks to reject the call.

"Aren't you going to get that?" I ask, surprised.

"I'm off the clock." Caleb grins.

"Really? I didn't think that was possible," I tease, only half-kidding.

He chuckles. "There's a first time for everything. I don't need to think about the office, not this weekend. I have everything I need right here."

Maybe it's another line, but I don't think so, not this time. And it's flattering to know that Caleb's put the rest of his high-powered life on hold so we could spend time together.

Maybe he really is serious about this second chance with me.

That decides it. If he's off the clock, then I am too. This weekend, Olivia and her secret suspicions don't exist. Nothing does, except Caleb, and me, and whatever he has planned.

And I'm betting it's delicious.

WE REACH the Hamptons in a couple of hours, and I watch as the rural beach towns shift into something more exclusive and grand. Here, the houses are massive and imposing, and the people we pass on the quaint cobbled streets are stylish, part of that wealthy country-club world that Caleb was born into. It's so foreign to me.

His hand rests on my thigh. "What are you thinking?"

"That we vacation in very different ways," I joke.

He chuckles. "What did you do for your summers?"

"Um. Hang around. Read. Lay out on the front lawn and get sunburned," I reply. "What do you do here?"

He grins. "Same."

Somehow, I doubt it. He stops at a crossing and my jaw drops as I glimpse a familiar face being hustled past by her bodyguards. "Wait. Is that Beyonce? I think that's Beyonce!"

He doesn't even look, so I try and regain my composure. I'm sure this place is swarming with celebs. I need to play it cooler than this before my head explodes.

I'm expecting us to head to a fancy restaurant or beach house, but instead, Caleb pulls up at a busy marina. "I thought we could take my boat out for the day," he says casually.

Of course he has a boat. No, a *yacht*. Complete with gorgeous white leather seats, polished mahogany trim, and even a little galley kitchen with an ice bucket and cold drinks waiting. Caleb gives me the tour, then sits me down to enjoy the view as he takes charge, unmooring from the dock, casting off, and unfurling the sail as we motor out of the marina.

And boy, is it a spectacular view.

I sit back, feeling the sun on my face and the breeze in my hair. Luckily, I dressed for the beach with a bikini under my denim cut-offs and loose blouse. As we pick up speed, I have to laugh.

Of all the ways I pictured spending my weekend, lounging on a luxurious yacht wasn't one of them.

"Having fun?" Caleb asks, glancing over from his spot behind the wheel.

"Maybe..." I tease.

"That sounds like a challenge to me."

Caleb motors us up the coast, and then drops anchor in a private little cove. He disappears into the galley, and re-emerges with a picnic basket. As he's setting everything out—strawberries and cheese and crackers and wine—I watch, impressed. "You plan ahead."

"I have help."

He pours me a flute of champagne, and I take a sip, even though I'm light-headed enough on my own. We sit, lounging on the comfortable cushions on the prow of the boat. I notice the ship's name emblazoned on some of the equipment. "Why 'Green Lights' I ask?"

"It was something my dad always used to say to my mom. 'Nothing but green lights ahead'." Caleb smiles. "My father was a hopeless romantic, right up until the day they died."

I remember reading how his parents were killed in a plane accident. I don't want to ruin the mood, so I just nod. "That's sweet. I love hearing great love stories. There's not enough of them to go around."

"Your parents didn't stay together?"

I shake my head. "My dad took off, a long time ago. My mom raised me on her own."

Caleb squeezes my hand. "My parents' relationship wasn't all sunshine and roses. In fact, they argued a lot. My father was busy with the company most of the time, and I know mom felt like she rarely saw him..." Caleb trails off. "But they loved me, I always knew that. It's ironic," he adds. "My mom hated to fly. She wasn't even going to make that trip with him, but I guess he convinced her."

"I'm sorry," I murmur, and Caleb gives me a rueful smile.

"Ancient history now."

"Still, it must've been a shock to you." I say.

"The biggest shock was inheriting the company." Caleb says, looking out at the ocean. "I never thought the responsibility would fall to me. At least, not so soon." He looks back at me. "But you must know a thing or two about that."

"Running a global jewelry empire?" I say lightly.

"No. Taking responsibility for your parent's affairs."

"Oh." I glance down, and nod reluctantly. "I've had time to get used to it, though. My mom didn't just wake up like this one morning. It was a slow decline. A blessing and a curse."

"How so?" Caleb watches me, his eyes soft.

"Watching her slip away from me, day by day... I wonder if it's harder this way, that's all."

He squeezes my hand again, and I shake my head, forcing a smile. "But thanks to you, I know she's safe, and well-cared for now."

"I'm glad I could help." Caleb says. "You shouldn't have to deal with it alone."

But I realize, I'm not alone in it, not anymore. And even if all Caleb ever does is sign the checks and hold my hand today, it's more than anyone else has ever done for us.

I smile, happy to just be here today.

Happy to just be with him.

WE TALK and eat for a while, just relaxing in the sun. I begin to feel the heat, so I start putting on sunscreen, slathering around the edges of my cover-up shirt. But as I'm trying to get sunscreen on the back of my neck, he sits down behind me.

"Wouldn't it be easier to take this off?" he asks, stroking at the flimsy fabric.

"Well... I'm kind of pale." I admit.

He chuckles. "It's June. You're allowed to be."

"You're not." I flash him an accusing glance.

He motions to the sunblock. "I'll put this on you. Don't be shy."

I look around, then throw off my cover-up, not sure if his

retinas are going to be forever burned by the blinding sea of white gooseflesh in front of him.

But he kneels behind me, and then I feel his hands on my shoulders, and the cool shock of the sunscreen.

He smooths it on, caressing.

"Is your goal in life to continually torment me?" he murmurs in my ear. "Because that bikini is hot. You might as well wear nothing."

I shiver in excitement as his hands keep stroking, beyond what anyone needs to do to put on sunscreen. His fingers dip below the ties of my bikini top, brushing my breasts, and I gasp.

"I should be thorough," Caleb continues, scooping more sunscreen into his palm. "We wouldn't want you to get burned now, would we?"

I silently shake my head, leaning back against him. His hands slide over my stomach, rubbing and teasing. His hand returns to my breasts, cupping them lightly, squeezing, gently pinching at my nipples.

I moan, feeling pleasure wash over me, hot as the sun.

Caleb leans in and kisses along the curve of my neck, as one of his hands strokes lower, between my thighs. He teases me through the fabric of my bikini bottoms, lightly rubbing my clit until I arch up against his hand, whimpering softly.

"God, you drive me crazy," he murmurs, and I have to bite back a laugh.

Crazy? He doesn't know the meaning of the word. Every touch makes my body taut with longing. Aching with desire.

He strokes again, lazily, then pauses. "You look awful hot around the collar," he says, teasing me. "I think you need to cool off."

Before I can react, he picks me up in his arms, strides to the edge of the boat, and leaps out into the ocean.

SPLASH!

The cold water closes over my head, shocking me. It's freezing! I sputter and kick back up to the surface. I break through, gasping for air, and splash water into his general direction. "That wasn't very gentlemanly!"

Caleb laughs, treading water beside me. "I never claimed to be a gentleman."

I splash him again, getting used to the temperature now. The cold is actually glorious against my hot skin, icy and refreshing. Caleb kicks over, and pulls me close, claiming my mouth in a kiss that's burning and cold all at once.

And utterly irresistible.

I wrap my arms around him and legs, and he keeps the both of us afloat there, treading water beside the yacht. I can feel his heart pounding against me. His solid torso, rock hard.

And the thick outline of him, pressing against me.

His hand dips below my bikini bottom, cupping my ass. I close my eyes. "You know what I can't stop thinking about?" His voice is a dark murmur in my ear.

I shake my head.

"That look in your eyes, right before you come. I want to see it again. Right now."

His hand slides lower, slipping two fingers inside me before I even know what he's planning.

Just like that, I'm impaled on his fingers.

I gasp, gripping his shoulders, trying not to sink beneath the water, completely under his spell.

The sun is shining above us and the water laps around us, but all I can feel is the thick invasion stroking me from the inside out. I tilt my head up, and he doesn't need me to say anything.

He kisses me, hard and hungry.

I lift my leg higher and wrap it around his waist, pressing

myself onto his fingers, shamelessly thrusting as he fills me up, thick and deep.

I moan as he dips his head, nosing my bikini to the side and sucking one nipple then the other, cupping my breasts and playing with them. It's like all feeling has centered where's he's touching me, and it's unbearable. He nips the hard bud with his teeth, and I let out a cry, digging my nails into his shoulders.

He lifts his head then, his gaze dark. "There. That look. You're close."

He shifts me, so my clit is pressed against him, the pressure driving me wild. I moan.

"Yes." Caleb growls. "Let me hear it again. As loud as you want, Juliet. There's no one to hear."

He rubs me up against his cock. Gently first, hitting all the right places. I can feel his heat, even underwater.

I can't help rocking on him. Harder, faster. The pressure inside and out so perfect, I'm mewling, my voice echoing out across the cove.

Caleb licks hungrily at my breasts. He holds me at the small of my back, letting me do all the work, sliding my crotch up and down on him. And that's fine with me.

Throwing my head back, I let out a moan. "Oh, god..."

I don't know when I start riding him with abandon, bucking up against him, my breasts bouncing, but soon, I'm barreling toward climax. When he thrusts a third finger inside me, my eyes meet his, and I wrap my arms around him and crash my mouth onto him as I come apart in his hands.

It's bliss.

16

JULIET

I THOUGHT that the orgasm would relax me.

I was wrong.

Oh, at first, I'm feeling relaxed, happy, as we hop in the car and head to his weekend place.

But then he turns into a winding driveway that leads to a sprawling mansion overlooking the ocean. The place is so big, the grounds so lush and manicured, at first, I think it's a resort.

But nope. It's all his. Well, his, and the coterie of staff that clearly keeps the place looking so gorgeous. Roses trail from the grey-washed shingles, the windows gleam, and every porch is set with a cozy bench or swing with perfectly plumped pillows. It's both casual and utterly intimidating all at the same time, the kind of understated luxury that takes money and taste to curate.

"*Sure*, you just sat around all summer growing up, sweating," I tease, reminding him of his earlier words.

Caleb smirks.

He pulls up out front and parks, then leads me through the front door. Of course, the place is incredible on the inside, too.

Everything is pale wood and soft textures, white and cream and blues to match the ocean beyond. Beyond the massive, sweeping staircase to upstairs, the whole back of the house is windows, offering a breathtaking view of the beach. "Wow," I sigh happily, taking it all in. Sure, I could try and play it cool, but a beautiful place like this deserves to be admired. I look around. "Are we the only people here?"

"Do you want to be?" He takes my hand and tugs me closer for a steamy kiss. I emerge breathless, my head spinning. He smiles. "I have my amazing kitchen staff preparing us dinner, but don't worry, they have the rest of the night off. I wouldn't want them hearing you moan," he adds, seductive, and I flush.

"I had them prepare a suite for you," he continues, leading me upstairs. He shows me to a room with a beautiful view of the water. "You should have everything you need. You can rinse off and change for dinner."

I pause, giving him a suspicious look. "You're leaving me to shower alone?" I ask. "No seductive lines, no trying to get in there with me?" I point my finger teasingly. "You have work you're sneaking off to do."

Caleb laughs. "Busted." He admits. "Just a couple of calls. But don't worry, you'll have my undivided attention for the rest of the night."

"Go." I shoo him, smiling. "Just think of me naked and soaped up while you're on those calls."

Caleb groans, but he leaves me to it.

I throw myself down on the massive bed and smile with satisfaction. To tell the truth, I'm glad to have a moment alone, to process everything that's happening. Caleb's presence is overwhelming. A force to be reckoned with. Like gravity, pulling everything around him into his path. And even though our afternoon on the water was tender and surprising in ways that I never expected, I still feel like I need to collect myself and come back down to earth.

He might not be the man I thought he was.

As I shower in the enormous bathroom, I can't help thinking about what Olivia said. *He'll use me, and then he'll cut me loose.*

A part of me has been braced for the bastard billionaire to return, but Caleb seems serious about showing me a different side of him. If he wanted to use me shamelessly for sex, he could have seduced me back in the city. We both know, I would have willingly let him. He didn't have to bring me here for a weekend together, spend all this time with me. Confide about his past, and find out about mine.

It's like I'm seeing his walls come down, little by little. The way he talked about his family, his fears, his burdens...

I slip on a long, strapless sundress and stare at myself in the mirror, a new warmth spreading in my chest.

Up until this weekend, Olivia had been right about everything Caleb did. I haven't doubted that she knows him far better than me.

But now, I have to admit... I'm starting to.

What if she's wrong about him?

What if she's wrong about everything?

DOWNSTAIRS, the house is quiet and still. The sun is setting, but I see lights flickering in the darkness outside, so I stroll out to the patio, where a candlelit table is overlooking the ocean.

Caleb is waiting for me there, looking absolutely irresistible in a white button-down shirt, the sleeves rolled up over tanned forearms. His hair is damp from the shower, and he's cleanly shaved, and when I move closer to greet him with a kiss, I catch the scent of his cologne again, the smell that seems to wrap around my senses. Intoxicating.

"Hungry?" he asks, and I nod.

It's the truth, after all. I just don't mention that I'm ravenous for *him*.

"Good. I had my chef prepare his special pasta," he says, pulling my chair out for me. "It's the best I've ever tasted outside Italy. I found him in a hole-in-the-wall place in Jersey, and offered him an arm and a leg to come cook for me."

"It looks amazing," I say honestly, taking in the spread. Pasta, salad, freshly baked bread rolls... I thought I was wound so tight, I couldn't eat a thing, but now I find I'm ready for a meal.

I tear into a dinner roll, as Caleb pours us wine. The cool evening breeze drifts around us, and the sound of the waves crashing against the shore plays a soothing soundtrack.

Maybe it's the setting, or the carbs, but I finally relax.

Tonight, nothing needs to matter except the two of us. Who knows when I'll have a chance to enjoy a date like this again. So, I let my nerves and anxiety fade away. Caleb seems more at ease, too.

He tells me more about his family, about the Hamptons, about how he used to spend his summers. He tells me that his father was always wrapped up in growing the business, and his mother was a bit of a social butterfly, so he spent most of his time with nannies, and at boarding school in Vermont.

"And going wild on vacation?" I ask, with a meaningful look. "I've seen the headlines."

Caleb gives a bashful smile. "My wayward youth," he says.

"So where does the Cross family come in?" I ask. We're leaned in toward one another, legs tangled under the table. "You were close?"

"They were like family, yes. Charles Cross was my father's best friend."

"And Olivia?" I ask carefully.

"We grew up together." Caleb takes a casual sip of wine. "She inherited half the business when they passed, but she's the social butterfly, so she usually handles our event schedule, the charity appearances. She loves all that."

I eye him. There has to be more behind this story. If, like Olivia says, he goes after every woman... Why hasn't he gone after her. "She's very beautiful."

"She is." Understanding must dawn at that moment, because he says, "We dated, briefly. Very briefly, years ago. But that was just two kids, fooling around. It wasn't serious," he reassures me. "Since then, we may have grown apart, but... She's like family. I'll always care for her."

I nod slowly. For the first time, I wonder how Caleb would react if he knew the truth. The real reason I came to work for him.

He misreads my silence. "Jealous?" he teases, and I shake my head.

"No."

Guilty.

He reaches across the table and takes my hand. "You should know, I'm not the kind of guy to keep things hidden," he says, tracing a circle on my palm. "There's nobody else, not right now. Only you."

I exhale in a shiver as he traces higher, up the inside of my wrist, and along my bare arm, all the way to my collarbone. His touch is like fire, igniting something deep inside me.

Desire.

"Are you ready for dessert?" he asks, eyes dark on mine.

I know, he's not talking about dinner anymore.

"Yes." I whisper. "*Please.*"

He smiles, but this time, there's an edge to it. A hunger I recognize. I feel it coiling inside me, too. Building, as he takes me by the hand and leads me back inside.

I follow him wordlessly through the house, and up the staircase. Anticipation builds, buzzing in my veins, as he leads me to his bedroom.

Plush rugs. Sleek furniture. Dark ocean views. I barely register a thing I'm so focused on him—and the epic king-sized bed in the middle of the room.

Caleb pulls me to him. He kisses me slowly, thoroughly, savoring my mouth until I'm weak and giddy in his arms.

"Do you trust me?"

I look up at him, at the promise of pleasure glittering in his eyes.

I slowly nod.

"Say it."

The order thrills me. The dark, dominant Caleb is back, and God, I love it.

"Yes," I whisper. "I trust you."

And I do: in here, at least. In this room, I know I can put myself entirely in his capable hands.

He's calling the shots.

He's completely in control.

Caleb crosses to the closet and produces two silk ties. "Come here."

I go to him immediately, and Caleb smiles at my obedience. "Good girl," he murmurs approvingly, and I feel another thrill.

I want to please him.

"Get on the bed," he tells me. "Lay back."

I do as he says. Caleb leans over and drops a burning kiss on my mouth. Then he takes my wrists, and pins them up above my head.

I inhale in a rush.

He smiles, carefully binding them together with one of the ties. "Look at you..." he muses, his eyes roving over me. "All tied up for me, like a Christmas present."

He loops the tie around a bar on the headboard, securing my hands in place.

Exhilaration floods through me. I test the bindings. They're taut, almost uncomfortable.

I can't get free.

Somehow, the knowledge that I'm completely at his mercy sends a rush of damp heat between my thighs.

I shudder.

Caleb dips a kiss to my temple, then produces the other tie. "Close your eyes," he orders, his voice silky, but absolute.

I do as he says, and then I feel the silk against my face. He binds it around me like a blindfold, the silk cool and pleasant against my burning skin.

Darkness.

My heartbeat seems louder, echoing in my ears as I adjust to the dim light. With my arms bound up over my head, and my vision gone, I feel more vulnerable than ever.

I can't move. I can't tell what he's planning next.

He has total control.

"Caleb?" I ask, my voice questioning.

He doesn't reply.

Then I feel the pressure of his touch suddenly, on my hips. The warmth seeps straight through the thin fabric of my dress. He runs his hands, strong and commanding, to the tops of my thighs. His fingers delve beneath my skirt, teasing. I shiver.

"Let's get this off you."

My dress ties at my shoulders. Caleb makes short work of the strings. He tugs it down over my body, a whisper of silk that's soon gone, baring me to the night.

And him.

I hear a chuckle. "No panties? You surprise me, Miss Nichols."

I smile beneath the blindfold. "Maybe you don't know me as well as you think."

Suddenly, I feel a pinch of pain: Caleb's fingers, tight on my aching nipple. I gasp.

"That's enough of your smart mouth."

I feel his other hand on my lips, silencing me. The touch turns to a caress, and then he eases my mouth open and slides his thumb between my lips.

The intrusion is so erotic, I moan.

"The only words I want to hear from you tonight, are '*yes, Caleb*'. '*More, Caleb.*' '*Please.*'"

"I..."

He plucks my nipple again, hard.

I gulp. "Yes, Caleb," I say obediently.

"Good."

His hands turn soothing, caressing. He skims over my body, stroking every inch of me for what seems like an hour. Teasing at the curve of my breasts, toying with my nipples, circling my stomach, and dipping between my thighs to brush across my clit.

I moan, arching into his hands, but it's never enough. The touch is so light, it's gone in a flash. Back down my thighs, over my calves, skimming back up again to—

There.

I moan louder as he probes the wetness at my core, nudging just inside me.

Not enough.

Another pet of my clit and then he's gone again, caressing my breasts until I'm sobbing with need.

This is heaven.

This is pure torment.

Over and over, he touches my body, bringing me to the edge of pleasure, but never far enough. Soft strokes, gentle touches, driving me crazy in the silky darkness, making me curse his name.

"Caleb…" I fight my bindings as he delves between my legs again, rubbing my clit in slow, hypnotic circles. "Caleb, *please.*"

"What's wrong, sweetheart?" Caleb coos, that note of pleasure in his voice telling me how much he's enjoying this.

My undoing.

"Please, I need you…"

"Need what, exactly?" Caleb pauses as I writhe. Dear God, he's trying to kill me.

"I need you," I manage. "Inside me."

He dips a finger into my wetness, flexes just once. "Like this?"

I clench hard around him.

"More. *Please.*"

"This?"

He adds another finger, thicker now, but he holds them so still inside me, denying me the friction I so desperately need.

"Please!" I'm sobbing now, scratching at my bindings, mindless, and I don't care.

He tuts, scolding me. "I've told you, Juliet. Use your words. I won't touch you until you tell me exactly what you want me to do to you." His hands leave me, empty and gasping. His breath is hot on my ear. "Say. Every. Word."

My body is pulled taut, humming with need. Something breaks inside me. I can't hold back anymore. Any last hint of shame or fear disappears in the face of my desperate craving.

"Fuck me!" I cry, shameless. "Fuck me, use me, do whatever you want, just fill me up. I need your cock!"

There's silence.

My stomach drops, dread creeps at the edges of my desire,

then I feel the mattress dip. Caleb's weight settles beside me. I feel his touch at my wrists, then suddenly, they're free.

He pulls my blindfold off.

I gasp.

He's naked there on the bed with me. Naked, and *magnificent*. I take it all in in an instant. The planes of muscular chest, the ridge of his abdomen.

His hard, straining cock.

Caleb rolls on a condom, and roughly parts my thighs. "There's no going back," he says, his eyes dark and intense on mine. "Once I claim this sweet cunt... You're mine. You understand? *Mine*."

I tremble out a nod, overwhelmed by the sight of him.

The promise of what's to come.

Then, without another word or warning, he thrusts inside.

I gasp, struggling to adjust to the thick invasion. He doesn't go slow, or wait for me to stretch around him.

Caleb holds me down and fucks me to the hilt.

Oh my God.

He fills me up, so deep I almost can't take it, but I have no choice. His hands are tight on my wrists, his weight driving me into the mattress, his mouth biting down on my shoulder in a sharp nip. He's everywhere, all around me, *inside me*. Totally overwhelming me. There's no room to think, or even breathe.

All I can do is take it, every last inch.

Fuck.

I'm still reeling when he pulls back, and thrusts into me again.

Harder. *Deeper.*

I cry out.

Pleasure is already rising in me, a thick sweetness I can't hold back. It's incredible, the feel of him, the wicked friction, sparking electricity in my veins.

"Goddamn, Juliet," he groans, rising up. His jaw is clenched. His eyes fierce in the moonlight. "Goddamn, you're so tight."

He thrusts again, and I clench around him, finding a rhythm now, rising up to meet him with every new devastating stroke. But just when I think I've found purchase, he shoves me down again. Hand on my chest, pinning me, helpless. Fucking me without mercy, without respite. Forcing me to take it however he chooses.

Forcing me to surrender entirely to the thick, relentless thrusting of his cock.

Over and over, he drives into me. Making me take every inch. Gasping. Moaning. Begging aloud. I don't even recognize myself anymore, I'm mindlessly sobbing, clutching at his back. Scratching, scrabbling, writhing in a slick mess as I cry out for him, so close I can taste it.

So close to the edge.

"Caleb!" I chant, arching up to meet him. "Oh God, Caleb!"

"Look at you, baby," he groans, watching me through lust-filled eyes. "Desperate for me. So sweet. So *wet*."

"Yes, oh God, yes!"

He keeps pounding, his thrusts deep and sure, and all I can do is let him. Plead for more. "You like that, baby?" Caleb commands. "You need it, don't you? You need every inch."

He slams into me again, and I howl with pleasure. It's cresting now, snaking up the back of my spine, holding me at its mercy. Aching for release.

"Don't stop," I beg him. "Please, don't stop!"

And he doesn't. he drives into me relentlessly, until I can't take it anymore. My orgasm rips through me, a crest of pleasure so strong it leaves me mindless, boneless in his arms. Caleb groans, clutching the sheets, and comes apart inside me, panting for air.

I lay there, stunned.

I've never known pleasure like this before, not even close. The other men... They're nothing compared to Caleb.

Nothing.

But now that I know what it's like to lose myself in his arms —lose track of everything except the exquisite pleasure and desperate, giddy release—I can't help but wonder.

How will I ever stand to be without it again?

17

JULIET

I WAKE on Sunday morning to bright sunlight painting ripples on the ceiling.

A shiver of excitement travels up and down the length of my body, as I remember what happened yesterday. The water. The blindfold.

The mind-blowing, earth-shattering sex.

I stretch, happily feeling the ache in my limbs; an echo of how far Caleb pushed me to my limits. I wonder what he has planned for the day. Something tells me, it won't just be browsing the Sunday newspapers and getting brunch.

No, Caleb Sterling would have more wicked things in mind.

I roll over, reaching for him—

But there's nobody in bed beside me. I roll over and confirm it. He's gone.

My stomach sinks.

Has he left, already? Was it all an act, after all?

Olivia's words come back to haunt me. '*When he gets what*

he wants... *Game over. He can't get away from them fast enough.'*

By surrendering to Caleb, have I rendered myself useless to him now?

Before my anxiety can whirl out of control, I notice a note on the bedside table.

On a run. Be back soon. – C

I exhale in relief—and then promptly feel embarrassed that I spiraled so quickly.

And that the rejection I felt wasn't just sexual.

Are you catching feelings?

I push the thought aside, and pull on a soft robe that's hanging on the closet door. In daylight, I can see that his bedroom is just like his place in New York—spotless, with few personal effects, giving little hint to the man that he is.

But I want to know more.

I wander out, and down the hallway, paying attention to my surroundings now. Curious, I peek into a series of immaculate guest rooms... Laundry... A gym... Downstairs, I find more signs of life. Framed artwork on the walls. Well-thumbed books and mementos on the bookcase. A ship in a bottle, a signed baseball in a case.

I come to a photograph and pause. It's Caleb and his parents, in front of the *Green Lights*. He must be about twenty in this photo—a bit gawky, not yet filled out like a man. His father could be his twin, except for his graying hair. His mother... she's a beauty. She's wearing a bikini top and loose pants, her skin sun-kissed, and looks almost like a young adult herself. Though they're smiling, there's something in her eyes that looks distant, not quite happy. She isn't looking at the camera—her eyes seem to be caught by something happening off to the side.

I stare at it too long. Eventually, I tear my eyes from it, peering in each room, until I come to an office. This one is cluttered with books, and some framed maps on the wall. Caleb's laptop is sitting there on the desk, open, the screen glowing.

My curiosity burns brighter.

I slip behind the desk and pull it closer, sure it'll be password-protected.

It's not.

All of Caleb's information is right there, waiting to be uncovered.

I hesitate there, my fingers on the trackpad. Should I do this? After everything we shared last night, it feels different now.

Maybe Olivia is wrong.

I deliberate a moment, then push the laptop away. It feels wrong to betray his trust here, in his own home. The office is different, but everything about this is personal.

Private.

More certain now, I make sure nothing is out of place, and turn to leave.

That's when I see it, on the ground.

The keychain I noticed in his office, the one shaped like a little globe.

I pick it up, weighing it in my hand. Then I realize it's not just a keychain. It's also a flash drive.

It must have fallen from the desk, without Caleb noticing.

What information does he store on it?

Suddenly, I hear the sound of the front door open, and then footsteps come in the hall.

"Juliet?"

Caleb's voice comes, calling for me.

Thinking fast, I hide the globe in the pocket of my robe and slip out onto the balcony, closing the doors behind me. It stretches around the back of the property, with access from every room. In a few short strides, I'm outside the living room—it looks as if I came directly from there, instead.

I lean against the railings, pretending to look out at the view.

"Out here," I call, sounding casual. A moment later, he steps out, joining me.

"Good morning." Caleb smiles. He's sweaty from his run: bare-chested and gorgeous. He pulls me in for a slow, sizzling kiss.

"It is, isn't it?" I smile back at him, chasing away my guilt. "Good workout?"

"It's a start." Caleb gives me a wolfish grin.

I laugh. "You have to keep up your stamina, I suppose."

"Speaking of..." Caleb yanks me closer again, hands roaming over my body inside my robe.

"You're all sweaty," I tell him, even though I love it. The raw, masculine musk of him.

"Then we better get me cleaned up."

Caleb takes me upstairs, and into his lavish bathroom. He turns on the shower, and promptly strips me naked, pulling the two of us into the steamy walk-in. The water jets pulse down on our bodies, and Caleb wastes no time at all getting me soaped up.

"I like to be thorough," he murmurs, his stubble grazing my bare shoulder as his hands sweep over every curve.

He kisses across my breasts, licking hungrily at the dip between them as the water runs down in rivulets over them. His hands slide up and down my torso, over the curves of my hips, coming to rest on my ass. He cups it, tempting me closer, until I can feel his cock against my lower abdomen, hard and ready for me.

I close my fist around him, marveling again at the thick

girth of it. He lets out a groan as I start to pump, finding a rhythm, soapy and slick.

Suddenly, Caleb pulls back. He spins me around and pushes me up against the shower wall.

"Hands up." He orders me, and I do as he says, thrilling at the steel in his voice.

I stand there braced, hands flat on the wall in front of me, cheek pressed to the cool marble. He nudges my legs apart, reaching around to possessively cup my sex, petting my clit and making me moan.

"Spread for me, baby," he demands, and I widen my stance. He pulls my ass back, angling me open, and then I feel the tip of his cock, demanding at my entrance. I brace myself, thrilled, ready for punishment.

This time, he sinks into me slowly. Inch by devastating inch.

I let out a ragged moan as little by little, he fills me up, burying himself to the hilt. His leans into me, his torso hot against my back, his hands roaming again, playing with my breasts as he starts to move.

Deep. Deeper. *Fuck.*

I gasp, braced against the wall, taking every thrust. He grips my hip punishingly hard, pumping into me, over and over again. The water beats down on us both, adding to the sensation, a dizzying rush.

Then he pulls back, and turns me to face him. "Now it's your turn," he growls, eyes dark with lust. He pulls us back, so he's sitting on the low ledge, and positions me above him, straddling his lap. "Ride me," he instructs, a sharp hand still at my hip. "Take what you want from me. Ride my cock."

I flush red, but the invitation is too good to resist. I sink down, taking him inside me, filling myself with his thick, unyielding flesh.

Dear lord, he feels incredible.

"That's right, baby," Caleb growls, holding me tightly. "Feel how deep I go."

I throw my head back, savoring every inch. *Fuck*, this new angle is something else, and straddling him like this, he hits places inside me I didn't even know existed.

"God..." I shudder, clenching tight around him. "I can't... I can't even move."

"Yes you can. I'll show you."

Caleb grips my hips and grinds me against him. The pressure hits my clit, and now the pleasure is everywhere. *Fuck*. I grind again, chasing that sweet friction. Raising myself up, and lowering to take him back inside me.

Caleb curses, his eyes dark. He thrusts up again, claiming my mouth with his lips as his cock pistons up inside me, thrusting his tongue between my lips, doing the same thing to my mouth with his tongue, as slowly and thoroughly as his cock does my cunt.

My breathing intensifies, becoming more and more ragged as he moves against me. I ride him faster, wanton now, shamelessly chasing my release as it builds, and coils, and slowly consumes me with need.

I whimper, loud, legs hooked tight around his hips and the friction of my nipples rubbing against his chest, almost too much, igniting the first of a thousand fireworks that pulse through me.

I tense and shudder, feeling it rise. Caleb grinds faster, thrusts deeper, and soon I'm bucking against him, coming apart, screaming his name as he rears up with a roar, pumping hard into me, so hard that I can feel it in every part of me.

I slump against him, trembling, and he holds me there against his chest, in the stream of the shower, until our breathing returns to normal.

"So, I take it you like the multiple jets?" Caleb asks, finally stretching. He's got a wickedly satisfied grin on his face, but I guess so do I.

I laugh, easing off him. "I like multiple everythings," I say, flirty. Afterglow is racing through my veins. I feel incredible.

Invincible.

Then my stomach lets out an almighty rumble. I flush, embarrassed, but Caleb just laughs.

"Sounds like we need to get you fed. After all, you're going to need your energy."

"Am I now?"

"Definitely."

IT ONLY TAKES us another hour—and two more orgasms—to finally dry off, get dressed, and drive into town. Caleb takes us to a cute, vintage diner that serves plenty of coffee and some amazing pancakes.

"God, these are good," I say, practically inhaling my plate.

"Hey now," Caleb teases. "I thought I was the only one who made you curse in pleasure."

I grin. "Well, you're not in my mouth now, are you?"

It's only after the words leave my lips that I realize just how filthy they sound. But Caleb does. His eyes darken, and he gives me a smoldering look.

"Careful now, Juliet," he says softly, that steel in his tone again. "Or I'll put you over my lap right here and spank you."

I shiver in delight. He would, even in front of a crowd. That's what makes his orders and authority so thrilling. It's not just talk, some guy acting like a big shot, making promises he won't deliver on.

I don't doubt for a moment Caleb would follow through.

We finish up, and Caleb reaches for his wallet to pay. Then he frowns, staring down at his hand.

"Need me to cover you?" I ask, teasing. "I could rustle up twenty bucks."

He gives an absent-minded smile. "Have you seen my keychain?"

Blood rushes to my face.

The globe.

"Isn't it right there?" I ask, trying to sound innocent.

"No, I mean, yes, but I keep a keyfob on the chain. A silver globe." Caleb frowns. "It's not here."

"Oh. Maybe you dropped it," I offer, thinking of where, exactly the globe is. Tucked in my purse, where I hid it after our shower sex.

"Maybe." Caleb keeps frowning.

"Or, it's probably back at the office," I suggest, feeling even guiltier. "I'm sure it'll turn up."

He nods. "Probably."

Which means I'll be getting in bright and early to plant it there, Monday morning.

Even so, I can tell he's tensing up again, as we hit the road, heading back into the city. With every mile we travel, his shoulders seem stiffen under my hand, and it's like he's already miles away.

"Earth to Caleb," I finally speak up. He glances over. "What's on your mind?"

"Hmm? Oh, nothing. Just stupid work things. I have a business trip this week," he adds, "So you'll have to hold down the office without me."

I feel a flash of disappointment that he's going—but also relief that I won't have to pretend like everything's purely professional between us at work.

I'm a terrible actress, and that? Would be an Oscar-level

role.

"Going anywhere fun?" I ask.

"Just London." He sighs, pushing a hand through his hair, and I have to giggle at the annoyance on his face.

"*Just London*," I echo. "Gee, I'm sorry your fabulous international travel is such a drag."

Caleb laughs, lightening up. "You're right," he says, smiling over at me. "I'm lucky. Still, it's no fun alone. Maybe you can come along next time."

He says it so casually, it's like he's inviting me out for dinner, but it takes everything I have not to squeal at the offer.

London?

He has to be kidding. Right?

I glance over, but Caleb is scanning through the Sirius stations, already distracted. "Well, have fun," I say, hiding my feelings. "Don't miss me too much."

"Oh, I will."

BACK IN NEW YORK CITY, Caleb drops me off at my apartment, and leaves me with a scorching kiss.

"Be good while I'm gone," he says, as he's leaving. "Otherwise, there's be trouble when I'm back."

I shiver, still beaming ear to ear as I let myself in my door. The kind of trouble I can't wait to taste.

"Tell me everything!" Kelsey greets me with an excited smile—and an expectant look. She's got a face mask on, and her hair drying in curlers. Just your typical Sunday evening attire.

"What do you want to know?" I ask, playing it coy. I dump my bag in my room, and saunter back to join her on the couch, kicking up my feet with a happy sigh.

"Everything!" Kelsey demands. "You waltz off without a

word, for the whole weekend. You were with him, weren't you? Ugh, you're so lucky I could scream. Was it good? Was he as skilled as everyone says he is?"

"Even better." I beam.

She shrieks in delight. "I hate you!"

"He took me to his place in the Hamptons," I add, loving the fact that for once, I'm the one with the wild romantic exploits to share. "We went out on his yacht and sailed around the bay. It was *amazing*."

"Bitch." Kelsey beams. "I can't believe it. How did he act?"

Kelsey peppers me with questions, and I recap the whole weekend, my smile getting wider as I recall every sexy detail. "Whatever anyone said about his... Skills in the bedroom? They weren't doing him justice. I've never come so hard in my life," I admit.

She sighs. "No wonder you're falling in love with him."

"Am not!" I protest immediately, ignoring the fluttering feeling in my chest that is definitely something more than lust.

"That's probably for the best," Kelsey agrees. "I'd hate to see you hurt."

"Oh, by the way, you got a delivery." Kelsey fishes a small box off the table and passes it to me. "More gifts from lover boy?"

"I don't know." I open it, curious, and pull out the package. It's a high-tech gadget of some kind. I squint at it, confused. It says something about downloading phone data?

"Weird," Kelsey says, looking over my shoulder. "Who's it from?"

I check the note.

*This should help you with his pho*ne.

"Olivia," I whisper.

Kelsey looks even more confused. "What's she talking about? Whose phone are you supposed to hack?"

I sink lower in the sofa cushions, feeling all the guilt and suspicion I've avoided come rushing back to the surface.

Phone hacking? Secret gadgets? What have I gotten myself mixed up in?

"Oh, Kelsey. I don't know what to do!"

"What does that mean?" She stares at me.

I sigh. "Remember how you heard Olivia talking about needing a good assistant? Well, it turns out, the job wasn't just logging Caleb's calls."

I quickly tell her about the *real* assignment: Getting close to Caleb and gathering evidence to prove he's embezzling from the firm.

Kelsey's eyes go wide. "He's stealing from Sterling Cross? But that doesn't make sense, he's already loaded."

I shake my head. "It's not like that. It's some kind of corporate theft, changing the official accounting and moving money around. At least, that's what Olivia says is happening."

"So is she right? Have you found any evidence?" Kelsey asks.

I pause. "He's definitely hiding something," I admit, not wanting to face the truth, but not able to avoid it all the same. "He has a secret second phone, and when he got a call on it the other night, he walked out on me in the middle of everything. Plus..." I reach into my purse and withdraw the globe keychain fob. "He seems really protective of this. He freaked out when he thought he lost it. I'm thinking maybe if there's any shady dealings... They might be stored on here."

She eyes it. "Why don't you look?"

"I'm afraid to." I admit. "I don't know if I want to find out the truth. He's going away for a few days, so I have that time to decide what to do. Maybe that, and distance between us, will give me some clarity on the situation?"

Kelsey eyes me doubtfully. "It seems like a no-brainer to

me, especially with Olivia's reward on the line. So if you're holding out... Maybe you are falling in love with him."

I hope not. Because that would make this complicated situation just about impossible.

18

JULIET

WITHOUT CALEB IN THE OFFICE, the week seems to go on forever.

I keep wrestling with what I'm going to do. *Look at the hard drive? Snoop in Caleb's things?*

Or ignore my suspicions—and Olivia's assignment.

Even though I decided to trust him out in the Hamptons, my time apart from him is making me reconsider. Without the haze of lust clouding my judgment, my doubts are coming to the surface again.

What if he's hiding something from me, something big? What if it all really is an act?

"...for the interviews and press rollout. Juliet?"

I snap back to reality, and find myself in the conference room, with a dozen faces looking at me. We're in the middle of another meeting about the upcoming anniversary gala, and I'm supposed to be taking notes.

"Right." I blurt. "Press passes and schedule. Got it."

"Great." David, who's leading the meeting, smiles. "That should just about do it. I won't keep you," he adds to the room with a smile. "I know it's rare to get a chance to work unin-terrupted."

There are chuckles. Everyone seems more relaxed without Caleb around barking orders, not just me.

Even if his orders are my favorite part...

I quickly check over the notes, and I'm relieved to find I managed to get most things on autopilot. I scold myself, adding a few extra details about catering and preview invitations. Caleb isn't even in the building to distract me. I should be able to do my job while he's gone.

The meeting ends, and I head back to my desk to type everything up. But despite the stack of work on my desk, I find my thoughts returning to one thing:

The little silver globe flash drive.

It's still burning a hole in my purse. If I'm going to slip it back in Caleb's office, it should be soon. But when I take it out, something makes me pause.

What if I'm letting desire blind me to the truth?

I was on board with investigating him before he seduced me. Olivia's concerns made sense. It was only once I met the man—and kissed him—that my resolve faltered. Just because he rocked my world in bed, that doesn't change the fact that some-thing has been going on with the Sterling Cross financials.

Am I refusing to see what's right in front of me?

Maybe it's nothing, I tell myself hopefully. Maybe if I check the flash drive, I'll find nothing but porn and online shop-ping receipts. After all, Olivia could be wrong. About everything.

But I have to know.

I glance around, checking that nobody's watching, then click it into my laptop, and pull up the drive. There's a pass-word prompt, and I stare at it for a moment before getting a flash of inspiration.

"It was something my father used to say... 'Nothing but green lights ahead'."

I type in the words with my heart in my throat.

Nothingbutgreenlights

It works!

The flash drive opens, revealing several folders. My pulse races. *Schedule. Contracts. Accounts...*

I click 'accounts' and bring up a number of spreadsheets. I open them and scan over the financial information. It looks familiar: I've seen them before. Victoria had me make endless copies just last week, to compile for the accounts report.

I exhale a sigh of relief. Nothing shady to see here. Everything's normal.

Except...

I pause over some of the totals, and open the file Victoria sent me to compare. I look from one to the other, and my dread returns.

The accounts are different.

Nothing major, just a different total here, for marketing expenses; and an extra line for a business loan repayment there. The accounts I printed and distributed look totally normal.

But the ones on Caleb's flash drive? The originals?

They show almost a million dollars is now missing from the company accounts.

But there must be a reason for it, right? Caleb will have an explanation, I'm sure. I just need to talk to him when he's back from London, and I bet everything will be straightened out.

"Hey, you hungry?"

I slam my laptop shut with a yelp.

"Woah, sorry to startle you." It's David, standing by my desk with a smile.

"Oh. Hi." I try to slow my racing heart. "Sorry, I was... Distracted. What's up?"

"Nothing much," he says, lingering there for some reason. He spots the sweatshirt on the back of my chair. "A Mets fan, huh?"

"Dyed in the wool." I smile.

"Me too! My dad took me to the ballpark every weekend," David says, grinning. "Lucky you're not a Red Sox fan, I'd never speak to you again."

I laugh, and we chat a little about sports, until we're interrupted by a messenger. "Delivery for Miss Nichols?"

"That's me." I accept the box. I pull out the card, and read: *Open this in private. – C*

I gulp. "I... Need to go." I say, jolting to my feet. "See you later!"

I bolt away from David, wondering what Caleb's sent me. Private... The only place I can think of is the ladies' restroom, so I shut myself into a stall, and then carefully open the luxurious black box.

Inside, I find a small, sleek bullet vibrator, with various straps attached. The diagram in the box shows that it's design to be worn inside my panties.

Inside *me.*

Excitement flares.

I'm wondering if I should put it on, when a text arrives on my phone.

'Wear it for me.'

That answers my question, then.

Heart racing, I lift up my skirt and peel down my pantyhose, and follow the diagram. The bullet is slim, and smooth inside me, but so small, I don't really feel a thing.

Huh.

A moment later, it emits a deep, low buzz that makes me shake from the inside out.

Holy shit!

I brace myself against the bathroom stall wall as the buzzing grows stronger. Harder. Igniting my lust and sending pleasure through me until—

It cuts out.

I catch my breath, gasping.

'Want some more?'

My eyes widen. Caleb's controlling the vibrations! Across an ocean, on a different continent, he's still found a way to drive me wild.

'*yes please*' I text back, and wait for the pleasure to start again, but there's nothing.

'Be a good girl, and maybe I'll let you have some more.'

I give a snort of amusement—and frustration.

So that's how he's going to play it. Still, it feels sexy to have a secret like this. I straighten up my clothes, and head out again, wondering when he's going to let me taste that pleasure. I cross the office, anticipating his move with every step. All the way to the lobby, around the block to pick up lunch at a café...

I'm waiting for him.

Wanting him.

As I'm waiting in line, I get a call from Olivia.

Talk about bad timing.

I let it go to voicemail, then listen after she's left a message.

"Juliet, hi, how are you?" she sounds friendly, but there's an impatient note to her voice. "Just checking in... I know Caleb is out of town this week, so I'm expecting you to be able to take a closer look at his affairs. We need to catch him in the act if the charges are going to stick. Remember, your reward is dependent on what proof you find. Call me!"

I gulp, feeling more conflicted than ever. When this whole thing began, nothing was more important to me than pulling off this assignment and getting the reward money for my mom.

But now everything's changed...

So am I dragging my heels because I don't need the cash any more, or because Caleb is winning me over?

I'm not sure, I just know that the data I found on the flash drive looks incriminating. But I'm not willing to hand it over to Olivia and sell him out without giving Caleb the chance to explain first.

I tuck my phone away, and approach the counter, about to grab my food to-go. But then I see someone waving from a table by the window. It's David.

"What a coincidence," he says, as I bring my takeout box over.

"You mean, that this is the best place to eat within two blocks of the office?" I tease.

He grins. "Why don't you join me? I could use your opinion on some of the anniversary plans."

"Me?" I ask, surprised.

"You seem to have good taste—in sports, at least," he jokes. "And maybe you can tell me what Caleb will hate, and save us both the trouble."

"Sure," I agree, and take a seat. But I've barely taken the lid off my salad, when I feel a sudden buzz throb through me, deep inside.

The vibrator!

I let out a yelp of surprise, clutching the table.

David looks concerned. "Are you OK?"

"Yup!" I blurt, as another buzz shudders through me. "Just a... Cramp."

"I'm sorry, I hate those," David says, sympathetic, and meanwhile, I have to clench to keep from moaning out loud.

He pulls out some publicity materials, and begins running through the different text options.

Another pulse vibrates.

I straighten. Cross my legs.

David pauses. "You think that's a good idea?"

I smile. No clue what he said. "Yeah. Sure."

More buzzing. This time, longer.

David continues, totally unaware. There's a break in Caleb's torment, long enough for me to catch my breath and recover, feeling human again.

Maybe that was just a preview, and he'll leave me guessing for the rest of the afternoon. Maybe—

Another deep throb rolls through me, like an ocean wave. On, and on, and—

Oh my God, I think I might come!

I push back my chair. "Be right back!"

I jump up and scurry away, face hot. David must think I have stomach problems. After a moment's panic, I finally find the ladies' room and dash inside, rushing past an old lady who is exiting.

My phone starts to ring. Caleb. I answer it, and desperately breathe his name.

"I want to hear you come."

I look around. The bathroom's empty, thank goodness, because I'm coming even before I get to the stall, my nipples tight, my body buzzing like a live wire. I let out a little moan as the vibrations get ever more intense, collapsing against the wall as pleasure rockets through me.

Oh. My. God.

I gasp, shaken and spent. "Bastard," I manage to mutter, and Caleb laughs down the line.

"Fuck, I miss you. Next time, you're going to be coming on my tongue."

· · ·

I DON'T KNOW how I make it through the rest of the day, but thanks to the time difference, Caleb heads to bed, and I can finally head home alone.

The things that man makes me feel, and he's not even in the room!

It's a marvel—and a liability. Because again, Caleb's sexual escapades have successfully distracted me from Olivia's demands, and the data I found on that flash drive.

I sigh, climbing the stairs to my apartment. One day soon, I know, I'm going to have to come clean—to one of them.

I'm just not sure which one.

I emerge from the stairwell, my keys out, but there's someone standing in the shadows by my door.

"Caleb?" I ask, my heart leaping. Is he here to surprise me?

But the man who steps into the dim light isn't Caleb. Not even close.

I freeze. He's massive, over six feet tall and built with lean muscle. Tattoos scroll down his arms, and there's a dangerous glint in his eyes. "Juliet Nichols?" he asks, taking a menacing step closer.

I back up. "Who wants to know?"

He closes the distance between us. I back up again, until I hit the wall. What do I do? There's nobody around, the dim hallway is totally empty.

Fear kicks, like ice in my veins.

I open my mouth to scream.

"I have a message for Caleb," he growls, towering over me.

I stare, wide-eyed. "C-- Caleb?" I stammer.

"Yeah. Tell him Nero Barretti isn't a man you keep waiting."

The words make me swallow my scream. He comes closer, closer... And right when I'm sure he's going to grab me, he sidesteps me and continues on his way down the stairs. Sauntering, hands in pockets, as if he didn't just issue that threat.

Every hair on my body standing on end, I rush for the door to my apartment.

It's open.

19

JULIET

"THIS SHOULD DO IT." The locksmith stands back, and then hands me a new key.

"Thanks." I gulp.

I spent the night alone, quaking in my bed, then first thing in the morning, called my super to send someone to change the locks.

Oddly enough, although the door was open, nothing inside was disturbed. That doesn't help me feel better. All I can do was think about that huge man, and his words: *Tell him Nero Barretti isn't a man you keep waiting.*

Caleb texted me last night, to tell me he was about to catch a flight back, but I didn't answer. I couldn't. I need to think.

Because now, I'm scared to death. Not just of this Nero guy —but the fact that Caleb seems to be mixed up with him.

What's going on?

I can't help wondering if this means that there's some truth to Olivia's allegations.

As the super's working, I hear Kelsey's voice out on the

stairs. She comes in, eyes wide. "What happened? Did someone break in?"

I nod, deciding not to tell her about our large visitor. It would only freak her out, and I'm freaked enough for the both of us. "I came back and found the door open," I explain. "But it doesn't look like anything was taken. Not that we have much to take," I add.

"Oh, my god! How scary," she says, shuddering as she gives me a hug. "And you stayed here alone last night? If you called me, I would've come back! I was just out at Jill's."

Jill is her younger sister. "I'm fine," I reassure her, even though I know I won't be sleeping for a week. "I'm sure it's nothing. Just some petty thieves." I check the time. "I've got to go. I'm late for work."

"OK, but call me if you need!" Kelsey insists.

Caleb's due back this afternoon, so the office is a buzz of activity, but Victoria is busy flitting between departments, which means I get a moment alone to think.

The first thing I do is pull my computer close bring up Google.

Nero Barretti.

There's plenty of hits about people called Barretti, but nothing I can see about a Nero.

Nero Barretti, NYC.

This time, I get more targeted results, but still, no Nero.

But I notice, there's a *lot* about someone named Roman Barretti. And it's nothing good:

Suspected Mob boss, Roman Barretti, 53, was arrested on suspicion of conspiracy over a multi-state drug trafficking ring...

I pull my screen closer, scanning the page.

The trial of Roman Barretti for numerous charges, from suspected murder to loan sharking, ended in a mistrial after the disappearance of several key witnesses...

Another trial against Roman Barretti begins today in New York, with the FBI boasting of a key witness inside his organization.

I scan the stories, a sick feeling growing in my gut, until I find the one word that confirms my suspicions: *Mafia.*

I stare at the page, a chill running down my spine.

Is the guy outside my apartment connected to this guy?

Did Caleb bring the Mob to my door?

Suddenly, there's a commotion in the lobby. I look up to see Caleb striding in, with an entourage. Victoria scurries alongside him, and half a dozen other people are clamoring for his attention.

"We need your sign-off on the designs..."

"I have the contract for your approval..."

"If I can get a minute for the Fall collection—"

They sweep past, and Caleb gives me a wry smile as he passes. "Looks like you all missed me," he jokes, giving me a wink.

They all disappear into his office. The door closes behind him.

I exhale in frustration, waiting for the meetings to be done so I can have a moment alone.

And waiting.

And waiting.

Finally, when the door opens, and another group of people march in, I can't take it anymore.

Mafia? Threats?

I need answers.

Now.

I take a deep breath, and go knock on the door. "Excuse me, everyone." I say, looking in. "But I need a moment with Mr. Sterling."

Caleb frowns.

"It's urgent." I insist. "It can't wait."

He nods. "Very well. We'll discuss this later. Victoria, set up the rest of my day. I'll need to touch base with every department."

She eyes me suspiciously. "Fine."

The rest of the group files out. I go in and close the door.

In an instant, Caleb is out of his seat. He pulls me into his arms, kissing me hard until I'm breathless.

"Impatient girl," he scolds me, with laughter in his voice. "You couldn't wait to have me, hmmm?"

I pull back. He thinks this is a seduction?

"No," I say loudly. I step away from him, far enough to think straight, and look him dead in the eyes.

"Who's Nero Barretti?"

Caleb goes still. "How do you know that name?"

His voice is like ice, eyes boring into me.

"Because he came to visit me last night. Or one of his friends did. I don't know. He broke into my apartment."

Caleb's expression changes. He grips my hands, urgent. "Are you OK? Did he hurt you?"

"No, I'm fine." I pull away. "But he said to give you a message. 'Nero Barretti doesn't like to be kept waiting.' What does it mean, Caleb? What's going on?"

Caleb clenches his jaw. "Nothing."

I snort. "Sure. nothing. That's why some tatted up Mob guy shows up at my door to threaten me. Tell me the truth. What are you into?"

"I said, nothing." Caleb barks. "I'll handle it."

"Handle what?" I demand, frustrated. "You're not telling me anything!"

"Because it's none of your business!" Caleb yells.

There's silence. I don't think I've ever seen him lose control like this. Never.

Caleb realizes it too. He takes a deep breath, and looks at me, cool and detached. The commanding CEO again.

"You don't have to worry about it. I'll have security put on your place."

My heart beats double-time. "Security? Does this mean I'm in danger?"

He doesn't answer, just stalks to the door and walks out.

I want to throw something.

Outside, I hear him telling Victoria that something came up and to cancel all his meetings.

And then he's gone.

I stand there, heart racing, surer than ever now that something is wrong. That in my lust, I may have completely misjudged Caleb Sterling. He's hiding something. Something big.

Something that's putting *me* in danger.

And there's no way in hell I'm going to stand by and wait obediently for him to figure it out.

I grab my purse, and follow him out.

20

CALEB

THEY CAME AFTER JULIET.

The thought haunts me as I stride down the street, elbowing my way through pedestrians on my single-minded mission.

I can't believe I let it get this far. They could have hurt her. *Or worse.*

A guy knocks into me, and I whirl on him. "Watch where you're going!" I bark, and he just laughs.

"Whatever, dude."

In a flash, I have him up against the wall, choking under my death grip.

"What... The fuck?" he garbles, gasping for air. I nearly pound his face into the concrete, but I catch myself just in time.

Pull it together, Sterling.

I step back, releasing him. He whimpers, and turns on his heel to run. I catch the looks of wide-eyed fear around me, and keep walking.

Attention is the last thing I need right now.

But anger drives me on, block after city block. Anger, and *guilt*.

Because I did this. I put her in harm's way. I thought I had it handled, but now, Nero Barretti is sending a clear message:

Nothing's off limits.

Nobody is safe if he decides to strike.

He's gone too far now.

I thought I'd do anything to protect my family's legacy. But it's nothing compared to the lengths I'll go to protect Juliet.

21

JULIET

I FOLLOW CALEB DOWNTOWN, my heart in my throat. Whatever he's up to, I have to know.

I'm not sure what I'm expecting, but somehow, I'm not surprised when I find we're back in that seedy neighborhood where I ran into him before. He ducks into the bar, and I wait on the street opposite, pacing.

Running through a thousand scenarios in my mind.

What is he hiding? And why won't he tell me what's going on?

Finally, after what seems like forever, he emerges, looking worn out. Our eyes meet across the street, and anger flashes on his face.

He strides over to me.

"What the hell are you doing here?" he demands, grabbing my arm. "Were you following me?"

"You didn't leave me much choice!" I retort. "You can't just leave me with no answers, and expect me to just go about my business like nothing's wrong!"

Caleb glances around anxiously, and then drags me around the corner. He pulls us into a deserted alley, out of sight of the street. "You don't understand," he swears through gritted teeth. "You don't know what you're sticking your nose into."

"So tell me!" I exclaim. "All this mystery, all your lies. I can't take it anymore. you need to tell me what's going on."

"Why? So you can put yourself in danger?" Caleb roars. "These are serious people. You need to leave it be."

"No!" I yell, furious. Then I catch myself, and take a step towards him, pleading. "Caleb, just tell me what's wrong. Is it about the business?" I ask, thinking of the flash drive, and those dummy accounts. "Are you doing something..." *Illegal? Are you stealing from your partner? Are you in league with this Mobster.* It's all on the tip of my tongue, but I can't get it out.

"I said I'll handle it." Caleb growls.

"And I'm just supposed to trust you?" I cry.

"Yes!" Caleb advances, backing me against the wall. "Why is that so hard to do?" he demands, breathing heavily. "Why can't you just believe me when I say, I'm trying to protect you! Please, Juliet..." His face cracks, and I see a terrible burden in his eyes. "I'm doing this for you. For everyone. You have to trust me. Please..."

I look at him, torn. I can see the desperation on his face. Whatever he's wrestling with, it's consuming him.

I want to trust him.

I want to believe that none of this matters. That the passion Caleb and I share is enough to paper over all these questions and make it all okay.

But it's not.

And this isn't just about emotion anymore. Sex, and the thrill of it, and our seductive dance.

That man threatened me. And whatever this business with

Nero Barretti, Caleb is in so deep, he can't even give me a simple explanation.

I pry myself from his grip. "I'm sorry, Caleb. You tell me to trust you... But I don't know if I can."

I race away, losing myself in the city streets until I'm blocks away, and can finally slow to a walking pace. I gasp for air, tears stinging the corner of my eyes.

What should I do?

My head is spinning with questions I can't begin to answer —and my heart aching with regret over the look I saw in Caleb's eyes. I wind up walking for hours,

turning it all over in my mind. I think of Nero Barretti's goon accosting me outside my door. Olivia telling me how I can't trust Caleb. But most of all, I keep thinking of his face when he told me to trust him... And the way it felt, sleeping soundly in his arms.

It feels real. The connection between us, the chemistry and the intimacy, too. We've opened up to each other, drawn by a passion I can't explain. That can't be a lie—can it?

Plenty of people have opinions about him. He's a playboy, a liar, a thief.

But do I believe them? Or was Caleb telling me the truth when he said he was trying to protect me?

Who is the real Caleb Sterling?

I go around in circles, playing everything back, over and over again. Our first meeting in the coffee shop. The reckless kiss in his office. That wild, erotic spanking session, and the weekend away, growing closer than ever.

My mom always told me to trust my instincts, and my instincts right now are telling me he has something to hide.

But they're also screaming at me to go to him.

That underneath it all, he's telling me the truth. He's trying to protect me. This isn't just a game to him.

Is it wishful thinking? Or does my body know something I don't? An elemental truth that all the doubt and questions in the world can't deny.

That I'm connected to him somehow. And if I have to take that leap, and trust *someone* in all this mess...

Well, there's only one person my heart is aching for.

I find myself outside his building. The doorman lets me up without a word. When the doors to the penthouse open, he's standing there, a tortured look on his face.

He doesn't speak, he just looks at me. Waiting.

"I do trust you," I say, holding his gaze. "Maybe that makes me crazy, but I do. I trust you, and maybe I'm even falling in love with you, and whatever it is you're hiding—"

He cuts me off with a wild, desperate kiss.

I melt against him, the passion surging through me in an instant. All doubts melt away under the intensity of his embrace.

This. This is what I trust. The way he makes me feel.

The pleasure only he can provide.

Caleb pushes me roughly against the wall. His mouth is devouring me, an almost animal power in every touch. His hands are everywhere, gripping me, squeezing. As if he can't live without me.

As if I'm the only one to soothe the beast inside.

I wrap my arms around him, clasping my hands around his neck and hanging on for dear life, lost to the passion, to his kiss. He grips my ass, lifting me, so my legs are wrapped around his waist and I'm pinned there, back against the wall. He shoves my skirt up, yanks my panties aside, and unzips in a breathless hurry.

I'm already wet. He's already hard. without a word, he buries himself inside me, all the way to the hilt.

I cry out.

Fuck, it feels so good. Like he's back where he belongs. Pounding into me.

Impaling me on his cock.

He holds still inside me, teasing me. making me ache. "Please, Caleb," I gasp, clinging to him. I clench around him, trying to draw him deeper inside. He slides his cock out, pausing when just the tip is still inside. His eyes lock on mine, dark with passion.

With possession.

Then he drives back in, forcing all the air out of my lungs.

God, it's even deeper this time.

His hands tighten on my hips, plunging into me, over and over. He grinds up, finding that sweet spot, making me moan and whimper with need.

"This is what you can't live without," he growls, slamming me into the wall with the force of his thrusts. "This is what you need, isn't it, baby?"

"Yes!" I gasp, arching against him to meet his thrusts. "Yes, Caleb, yes!"

It's wild and reckless. Beyond reason or sense.

"Because I own you." Caleb grips my jaw, holding my head in place. Forcing me to meet his gaze. "This body. This sweet cunt. It's mine now. There's no going back."

The look in his eyes is ravenous. Raw. It ignites a new fire inside me.

"I'm yours," I cry, mindless with pleasure. "All yours!"

He pistons again, and the pressure of his pelvis grinding on my clit is too sweet, too much. I'm on the brink of oblivion again. Every nerve inside me is tingling, so I grasp his shoulders tighter, digging my nails into his back.

"Mine."

Caleb comes with a roar, as my climax rips through me. Pleasure crashing, over and over, turning me inside out.

Turning my world upside down.

As I come down, I know that what he said was true. It's the two of us, in this together.

Now, there's no going back.

22

JULIET

I WAKE the next morning to the smell of something delicious wafting through Caleb's apartment. Is that... ?

Bacon.

I sit up, yawning, feeling content and satisfied in a way I never have before. The night passed in a haze of soft whispers and hard pleasure; now that I've made the decision to trust him, everything has fallen into place.

We belong together.

"Good morning," Caleb says, strolling into the room. He's carrying a tray with an incredible breakfast spread. "I hope you're hungry."

For him, yes. My nipples tighten and I can't help the heat that floods between my thighs. "Since when do you make your girls breakfast?"

He smirks and brings the tray closer. He says, "Trust me, there's never been anything quite like you in my bed."

I blush,

focusing on the array of breakfast pastries, eggs, bacon,

freshly squeezed juice. But in the back of my mind, a voice is whispering.

Trust goes both ways.

I have to tell him about Olivia.

Soon. But not now. He settles the tray on the bed between us, and pours coffee from the French press.

"Mmm..." I relax happily, nibbling on a slice of bacon. "Now this is the perfect way to start the day."

"I'd say so." Caleb gives me a wolfish grin, his hand sliding under the covers to my bare hips.

I giggle, batting his hand away. "Food first," I pretend to scold him. "I need my strength."

"Good point." Caleb digs into the eggs, unfolding a newspaper that's resting on the tray.

I look over his shoulder, and notice a feature on Sterling Cross's anniversary gala this weekend. "Are you sure you have time to lounge around with me?" I ask. "There must be a ton of work to do, preparing for the event."

Caleb gives an easy shrug. "I'm sure they can handle it. Besides, I'd rather spend the day with you."

I flush happily. "I want to spend time together too. It's just... " I pause. "I usually visit my mom today. She'll be expecting me."

If she can remember who I am, that is.

Caleb nods. "I'd be happy to drive you."

"Are you sure?" I ask. Visiting a residential home isn't exactly thrilling date material.

"Of course. I'd love to meet her. if you're OK with that," he adds.

"Oh. Then... Yes." I smile, nodding. "I'd like that, too."

I EXPLAIN to Caleb about mom's favorite treat, so we stop and pick up a box of bear claws as usual, before heading out to Meadow View. I feel nerves tangle in my stomach as we park and head inside. I've never brought anyone here, and I can't help hoping that mom is lucid enough to meet Caleb.

Luckily, her favorite nurse greets us with a smile. "She's in a good mood," she remarks, leading us down the hallway. "She's been sitting out on her patio every morning. She just loves the flowers."

Patio?

I frown, confused, especially when we reach her room—and I see it's empty. I look around.

"Where are all her things?" I ask.

Ann looks surprised. "In her new room. That was your instruction, wasn't it? The best room in the building."

I look to Caleb, who has a knowing smile dancing on his lips. "You knew about this?" I ask.

He squeezes my hand. "I may have called to see if there was anything we could do to make her more comfortable. They mentioned she enjoyed the gardens, so it made sense for her to have a private patio."

I want to throw my arms around his neck and kiss him, right there in the hallway.

"Thank you," I mutter, squeezing back.

We follow Ann to a part of the building I didn't know existed. This section is plusher, brighter, and homier. "She's right in here."

Ann directs us into a room that must be twice the size of her last one, decorated in cheery yellow tones. And the light! Everything is bright and sunny, and she even has a little seating area off the main bedroom with a couch and comfortable chairs. There is a pair of French doors ajar, leading outside, and when I step out, I find her on a small patio overlooking the gardens.

She's pottering around, watering some herbs that are growing in colorful tubs.

"Hi, Mom!" I say brightly, hoping and praying that she'll remember me.

She looks over and smiles. "Juliet. I was just thinking about you. The basil is coming in so nicely, remember that pesto recipe you always loved?"

My heart swells. It's just a simple memory, but it means so much that she can hold onto it, even for a little while.

I rush over and give her a massive hug. "I missed you," I choke out, before getting myself under control. "I brought you something."

Caleb steps in, and my mom's eyebrows shoot up. "All this, for me?" she asks, teasing.

I laugh.

"Actually, the pastries are for you," Caleb says, holding out the box. "I'm already taken."

"This is Caleb." I introduce them. "He's . . . My . . ."

Oh, god. What is he? *Boss* isn't right. Not anymore. *Boyfriend* is too sixth-grade. And *lover?* Nothing can bring me to say that in front of my mother.

He comes forward and shakes her hand. "Hello, Ms. Nichols. Lovely to meet you," he says with his effortless charm, and the issue is forgotten.

She beams. "Goodness. Aren't you handsome?" She winks at me.

"Mom!"

He laughs. "It's quite alright. Can I get you ladies something to drink with those pastries? I saw a coffee machine on my way in."

"Thank you."

He leaves us to it, and I take a seat beside mom, watching

her tend to her plants. "Well..." she says, giving me a knowing look. "No wonder you look so happy."

"Do I?"

"Of course. It's written all over your face. You can't hide love," she adds, smiling.

Love...

I let out a shiver of breath. It's been dancing around my mind all day, but I'm not ready to admit it to myself just yet. "It's... Complicated," I tell her, but mom just smiles.

"Love is simple. Everything else? Well, that can get messy. But you always know in your heart what's right." Mom pats my hand. "The trick is, listening to that voice inside, instead of all the noise around you."

I smile, overwhelmed with emotion. To be sitting here, talking like normal... it's something I never take for granted. Because every moment of clarity is a gift I might never get back.

Caleb returns with our drinks, and we all sit, eating and talking. I wish I could stay forever, but Ann eventually interrupts us. "It's time for her therapy session," she says, regretful. "It's really important for her treatment."

I nod, getting to my feet. "I'll see you soon," I promise, hugging her tightly again.

"Of course you will." Mom smiles. "And I'll hope to see you, too," she adds to Caleb. "Take care of my girl."

"I will."

I'm quiet as we leave. It's bittersweet. It was wonderful spending time like this with her today, but I know, it might not happen again for a while.

Caleb seems to understand. He leaves me with my thoughts, and when I look up, I find we've come to a stop, parked on a street beside Central Park.

"How about we take a walk?" he suggests.

"That sounds perfect."

It's a gorgeous day, a brisk Spring breeze in the air, and we walk for hours, just talking together about everything under the sun. It seems like a weight is off his shoulders, too. He's smiling, and laughing, a different person to the tense, angry man who exploded last night.

Maybe he was telling me the truth. Whatever the problem was, he's handled it.

We get hot dogs from a cart, and, sit at a bench at the Alice in Wonderland statue, soaking up the rays.

"Delicious," I say, wiping mustard off my chin. "Never mind all the fancy hors d'eurves, we should serve these at the gala tomorrow."

Caleb laughs. "I'd love to see their faces if I did. Olivia would probably flip a table."

Olivia.

Just like that, my good mood sours.

Because Caleb isn't the only one with secrets, and mine isn't behind me. Not even close. I came into his life under false pretenses. Everything we have is built on a lie.

Do I have to tell him? Or could I do what he's done: Leave that all in the past, and move on. No questions asked.

Could I live with that kind of lie?

"Listen, Caleb..." I start, then stop again. How can I even explain myself?

And what would he say, if I came clean?

He looks at me expectantly.

"Nothing," I deflate, chickening out at the last second. "I was just

thinking about the gala tomorrow," I lie.

"Me too." Caleb says. "Would you come?"

"I'll be there." I nod. "Victoria's given me a whole list of work to do, I'll be running around behind the scenes all night."

"No," Caleb says, smiling at me. "I meant, come with me. As my date."

I stop in my tracks. "Are you serious?" I ask. "Because that would mean... Being together, in public. Officially."

"I know." Caleb nods. "I don't want to sneak around anymore. I want the world to know, I'm serious about you. No more secrets."

I catch my breath. He wants to tell everyone that we're together. That I'm the only one he wants. It's amazing, and overwhelming and—

Real.

And I know now what I have to do. If we're going to have a future together, I have to make this right.

23

JULIET

THE DAY of the gala is all hands on deck. This is the biggest event that Sterling Cross has ever hosted, and it's the hottest ticket in town: The event's at the Plaza hotel ballroom, there'll be a red carpet with the world's most famous celebrities—all wearing the brand's finest pieces—plus press, social luminaries, corporate partners...

All eyes will be on the company, so it's no wonder every staff member is working overtime on a Sunday, making sure everything goes off without a hitch. I barely see Caleb all day, but he sends me a text.

Pick you up at six.

I swallow my nerves. "OK if I take off now?" I ask Victoria, an hour before showtime. "I need to change for the event."

I haven't told her I'll be walking in on the CEO's arm. I figure that's a surprise better left until the last minute.

"Did you coordinate with the catering company, and double check the seating charts?" she demands, looking stressed.

"Yes," I tell her. "And I also took care of a few more things on your list." I pass over the stack of pages, detailing all the extra details. "You looked like you could use the help."

"Oh." Victoria blinks, surprised. "Thank you. I suppose you could duck out now," she says grudgingly. "You'll need to clean up, we have to set a tone."

That counts as a favor, I guess, so I don't ask twice, I grab my things and get out of there.

But I don't go home.

I head to the Upper East Side instead. To Olivia's townhouse.

Standing on the steps, I brace myself—just like the last time I was here.

The butler answers and leads me to the front room, where Olivia is standing on a dais in front of a floor-length mirror, in a blinding golden gown. A small seamstress is scurrying around the platform, straight-pins between her lips.

"Juliet!" Olivia beams, spotting me in the reflection of the mirror. "How are you? I was just thinking we should have a talk before the gala. To get on the same page. Sit."

I don't sit. I suck in a breath. I force my voice to stay steady. "Olivia. I came here to tell you—"

"Maybe a little more leg?" she interrupts, studying her reflection. "It is a party, after all."

"Of course, Miss Cross."

I clear my throat and try again. "Olivia. We really need to talk. About our... Arrangement."

I eye the woman, and Olivia seems to realize something's wrong. "Of course," she says. "Magda, would you give us a moment please? There are refreshments in the kitchen."

The seamstress makes a polite exit, leaving us alone.

"Good idea," Olivia says, stepping off the dais. "We need to keep this confidential, until all our ducks are in a row."

I swallow hard. "There won't be any ducks," I say. "I mean, I can't do this anymore."

Olivia freezes. "What are you saying, Juliet?" She turns, giving me a searching look.

I glance away. "I can't help you find evidence against Caleb, because there's nothing to find. He cares about Sterling Cross, your families' legacy. Whatever he's doing, I'm sure it's in the best interests of the company." I say quietly. "And what you're trying to do here... I don't want any part of it."

"Are you kidding me?!" Olivia's voice echoes, harsh and furious.

I step back, shocked by the vitriol in her eyes.

She takes a breath. "I just mean, what happened?" she asks, smoothing her dress down, collecting herself. "You told me, you had suspicions. The phone calls, his behavior. What changed?"

I look down.

"Oh." Realization dawns. "He's seduced you. I should've known."

"It's not like that," I protest, even though it's true. But not the whole truth. "I've gotten to know Caleb. He's a good man."

"You mean, he's a good fuck." Olivia rolls her eyes. "I get it, I've been there," she adds. "But you can't let that cloud your judgment. He doesn't mean any of it. Not a single word. I know him, Juliet," she insists. "He's a liar, and anything he's saying to you, promising you, isn't real. That's a fact."

"I'm sorry," I whisper. "Maybe you're right, but I'm not spying on him any longer. I won't help you anymore."

Olivia shakes her head sadly. "You're making a mistake, Juliet. He'll break your heart. Mark my words."

Maybe. Maybe he will. But as I leave her house, I can't help feeling lighter. Olivia's games are behind me now. And once I come clean to Caleb about everything...

There'll be nothing standing in our way.

∽

BACK AT MY APARTMENT, I'm hunting in my bag for the keys when Kelsey throws the door open. "Oh." I stop, blinking in surprise. "What are you doing back from work so soon?"

"I'll tell you later," she says. "But for now, you have a few visitors."

Our apartment isn't the biggest. We even had trouble fitting our two-person couch in the living room. Right now, it's so packed with bodies, it looks like a Saturday night rave. "Who are these people?" I ask, confused.

A woman with blonde curls says, "We're here to help you get ready for the gala. Hair, makeup, wardrobe." She points around the room.

"Is this all necessary?" I ask, hesitant.

The woman gives me a look. "Mr. Sterling said you might try and send us away. Believe me, all eyes are going to be on you tonight. You're going to want to look your best."

"If you think that's over-the-top, check out what's on the table," Kelsey adds.

I go look. There's a massive box, from a designer brand I can't believe. And inside, there's a stunning strapless black ball-gown. Elegant. Chic. Timeless.

And mine.

I feel a thrill of excitement. They're right. This is a big night, not just for me, but for Caleb, too. I know how hard he's worked, and I want to do him proud.

"OK," I say, turning to the team. "Let's do this."

I hop in the shower, and then let the glamming commence. It always looks like fun in the movies, but I soon find out, it's like being caught in a rather uncomfortable storm, people prodding and poking, curling and painting. But when they finally stand back, the woman staring back at me from the mirror looks like a million bucks.

"Wow," Kelsey says, watching me. "I guess this is what money can buy."

I turn, confused by the edge in her voice.

"You look great," she adds quickly.

She smiles again, but it doesn't quite meet her eyes. There's something off with her. She's normally so upbeat. I wonder if she's a little jealous, but I guess I would be, too, if I were in her shoes.

I give her a hug. "Next time, you'll be my plus-one," I tell her. "In fact, I'll insist of it. And I have some pull with the CEO," I add with a wink.

She smiles again, for real this time. "Knock 'em dead."

There's a knock, and then Caleb is standing in the doorway, looking hot as ever in his tuxedo.

"How many of those do you have?" I ask, amused. "Or do you keep black tie outfits the way I keep old jeans?"

He doesn't reply. His eyes are drinking me in, and there's a new expression on his face. Almost reverent.

"You look beautiful," he says simply, and I melt.

"I had help," I say, gesturing around. "Thanks for that, by the way."

"Any time."

Caleb reaches into his pocket and pulls out a long jewelry box. "We're auctioning this off tonight for charity. It was supposed to be in the displays but I can think of no better way to show it off. I wanted to see it on you one last time."

He opens the box, revealing that incredible diamond choker.

He lifts it out, and fixes it around my neck, fingertips brushing my skin and sending shivers through me. "I have fond memories of this necklace," he murmurs in my ear.

I blush remembering the last time I wore it. *Wore nothing but it.* On my hands and knees, begging for his touch.

"There. Perfect." He stands back, and offers me his arm. "Ready?"

I take a deep breath, preparing for my first public event with Caleb Sterling.

"Ready."

24

JULIET

EVEN THOUGH I'VE seen the plans for every detail, nothing prepares me for arriving at the gala as a guest. We pull up outside a red carpet stretched all the way to the lobby, and take our places walking amongst all the glittering guests; Caleb smiling and nodding at people as we pass. Photographers flash their cameras, making me see stars, and I grip his hand tightly, already feeling way out of my depth.

"I'm sorry," Caleb murmurs, sweeping me inside. "I would have us slip in the back, but I need to play host for the night."

"I understand," I give him a smile. "This is your night, after all."

"For my sins," Caleb murmurs cryptically, as we step through the lobby and into the main ballroom. It's gorgeous: Lavishly decorated with an Art Deco theme, full of crystal chandeliers and golden fixtures. With the addition of the Sterling Cross items up for auction, adorning the display cases on the wall, the place simply sparkles.

"Are you nervous?" he asks me, and I have to wonder what gave it away. My sweaty palms? My flushed skin?

"Obviously."

He kisses my knuckles. "Don't be. You're the most beautiful woman in the room."

I blush again. "Listen," I say, feeling a pang of guilt. "We should talk later... After the event."

"I agree." Caleb smiles. "Come on. I'll introduce you to some important people."

We weave our way through the crowd. People stop what they're doing to watch or greet him as he passes. He's the man of the hour, full of charm, but doesn't break stride until he pauses in front of a white-haired, well-dressed couple.

He kisses the woman's cheek, who beams at him, and shakes the man's hand. "Edith and William Delacort were some of my parents' greatest friends," he says to me. "Let me introduce you to Juliet. My girlfriend."

"Oh!" Edith says, surprised. And she's not the only one. Something tells me, from the way she appraises me carefully, that he doesn't do this often. "Lovely to meet you, dear," she says, greeting me. "I hope to see more of you. Perhaps at the opera next month? We have a box we barely use, but we'd love to host you both."

"That sounds great," Caleb says, his arm slung casually around my shoulders. "Let's set a date."

My thrill grows. Girlfriend... Plans... He really meant it when he said he wanted to make this official. He takes me to meet more people, and with every new introduction, my confidence grows. I can see people sizing me up, but I stand tall beside him.

Tonight, I feel like I really belong.

After a while, the blur of new faces gets overwhelming. "If you'll excuse me," I say politely, glancing around for a restroom. "I'll be right back."

"And I'll go find us some drinks," Caleb says with a wink.

I slip away to the ladies' room. It's a cool marble sanctuary, and I take a moment alone to collect myself, running the cold faucet over my wrists to calm down.

It's a lot, being the one on his arm. I just hope I'm rising to the challenge.

I check my reflection, and touch up my lipstick. Some of my hair is trailing from the complicated twist the hairstylist constructed; It's snagging on the diamond choker, pulling it slightly off-center, so I unclasp the necklace to reposition it again.

But when I look closely, I notice something.

The inscription I saw on the inside of the necklace, the one that said *Petal*?

It's gone.

I inspect it closer, sure I must have missed it. But no, the etched letters aren't there.

This isn't the same necklace.

I feel a chill. Caleb said it was one-of-a-kind. So what's going on?

Quickly fastening it back on, I head to the ballroom, looking for Caleb. I scan the crowds, finding him talking with another distinguished-looking man. I hurry over to them, and force a smile. "Can I steal you for a second?" I ask Caleb.

"Duty calls." He tells the man.

I draw him away from the crowd, to a private alcove. "Caleb, I think there's something wrong with the necklace," I tell him, pressing a hand to my throat.

"What do you mean." He looks at me, wary.

"It doesn't have the inscription. I think it might be a fake!"

"Shh," Caleb hushes me immediately. He looks around. "You can't say something like that, not here."

"But—"

"You're mistaken." He shuts me down, voice firm. "There's

nothing wrong with that necklace. I fetched it from our vault myself."

I frown at him, wondering what the hell's going on. But before I can press it any further, a tall, impeccably dressed man saunters up.

"Lovely shindig, Sterling," he says, in a crisp English accent. "You've got a future as a party-planner, should you need a new direction in life."

Caleb's eyes turn icy. "I didn't realize they were letting anyone in."

"I pulled some strings. Wanted to see the big event for myself. End of an era, isn't it?"

Caleb frowns, looking thrown, as the man turns to me and offers his hand.

"Sebastian Wolfe. Charmed, I'm sure."

Wolf. The name suits him. There's something predatory behind his gaze that makes me shift, uneasy. I take a half-step back, closer to Caleb. "Hi." I say politely. "Have a lovely evening."

"Oh, I will." Sebastian looks around, smug. "I just wonder how these people will react when they hear the news that I'm acquiring the company."

Caleb stares, hard. "Over my dead body."

As smooth as can be, Sebastian takes another sip of his scotch and says, "I'm sorry. I didn't think you had a say anymore. Now that you're being kicked out for fraud and theft."

My heart jams in my throat, making breathing impossible. *Fraud and theft?*

The same things that Olivia hired me to...

Oh, no. It's not true.

Caleb glares, his usual composure slipping. "What the hell are you talking about?"

"Caleb…" I try to get his attention, as I notice Olivia, in her golden gown, sweeping across the ballroom. She has an entourage of suited men in tow, and a determined smile on her face.

A smile that says that she got all the evidence she wanted.

No.

Caleb strides to meet Olivia in the middle of the floor. "What have you done?"

"Only what needed to be done." She looks around at the curious onlookers, "Perhaps we should talk in private, away from the party, so we can avoid any unpleasantries?"

I can tell Caleb is torn, but he gives a sharp nod. He follows the group down a hallway, into a side room. I trail behind, sick to my stomach.

What does Olivia have on him? I didn't tell her a thing, but clearly, she's on a mission. And how does Sebastian Wolfe connect to any of this?

Away from the crowd, Caleb whirls on her. "Will someone please explain what the fuck is going on?"

"Don't play dumb with me." Olivia's voice is sharp. "You know exactly what you've done. And now the whole world will know too, you're nothing but a common thief."

She produces a sheaf of papers, and places them smugly on the table.

"Copies of your dummy accounts—and the real deal. It's all here. All the evidence that shows you've been moving money around. Embezzling from the company our parents built. This illegal activity means that you're to be removed from your CEO position and seat on the board at once."

"The board…" Caleb stares at her. "Fuck, this is what it's all about. You want me removed, so you can force through the plans to sell the company. Christ, Olivia how could you think about betraying our parents' legacy like this? After everything they sacrificed—"

"*They* sacrificed?" Olivia's voice rises, color sharp in her cheeks. "They sacrificed nothing! I was the one left alone, to be raised by nannies, and shipped off to boarding school because they cared more about a bunch of dumb rocks than their own daughter! They gave everything to this company. Not to me! They even died for it! So yes, I want to be shot of this place. I want to sell out, and take my mountain of cash, and never have to look at another fucking Sterling Cross logo ever again!"

Her voice echoes, sharp with rage.

And I realize with a sinking heart, that I've been played.

She was never worried about protecting the company. She didn't care about the embezzlement, not really. All she wanted was a reason to remove Caleb from his CEO position, so she could destroy the company she's clearly loathed all her life.

And I helped her do it.

Caleb turns to leave. "Your little plan will fail," he tells her, furious. "My people will block any attempt to unseat me. You can't prove anything."

"Oh, you covered your tracks pretty well. It was almost impossible to find those fake accounts," Olivia says proudly. "But we found your secret dummy files."

She pulls something out of her purse, and dangles it from one finger. The silver globe flash drive.

I gasp—at the same time Caleb does. "How did you get that?" he demands.

"Thanks to Juliet here." Olivia beams.

"*Juliet?*" He freezes.

My heart stops.

"She got it for me," Olivia says with a smug smile. "Why do you think she wound up in your office? I hired her from the very beginning, to keep an eye on you. A close eye. She was very effective, wouldn't you say?"

Caleb looks at me in disbelief. I feel sick. "It's not like that!" I protest. "I didn't give her that drive." But Olivia just smirks at Caleb, enjoying her victory.

"You always thought you were the smartest man in the room, but you didn't see this, did you? Your little girlfriend was willing to sell you out, and you fell for it. Hook, line, and sinker."

"No!" I cry, moving to Caleb's side. "She's twisting everything—"

But he wrenches free. Gives me a look so cold, it could freeze an ocean. Then storms out.

I rush after him, panicking. I have to make him listen, make him understand, it's not like it sounds.

I catch up with him in the hallway. "Wait!" I call, desperate. "Caleb, wait!"

He whirls around.

"Is it true?" he demands, searching my face. "Did Olivia hire you to spy on me?"

"Yes, but... I didn't betray you. I promise!" I grip his hand, imploring. "I didn't know you in the beginning, and I needed money, for my mom. But when I got to know you... Everything changed. I told her, tonight, I wouldn't do it. I swear."

"Then how did she get my flash drive? You took it, didn't you?"

"Yes!" I blurt, helpless. "But I didn't give it to her, I swear. I never wanted to hurt you," I add, desperate. "I love you!"

My voice echoes in the empty hallway, and I stand there, holding on to him, willing him with everything I have to believe me.

Caleb wrenches away.

"That's enough," he says, cold as ice. His gaze flicks over me. Like I'm a stranger.

Like he's already forgotten my name.

"You've taken everything from me, Juliet," he says slowly. Making each word clear. "My reputation. My company. My family's legacy. But whatever she paid you, I hope it was worth the price. Because you don't know what I do to my enemies. But I swear to you, you're about to find out."

And with that final devastating promise, he walks away from me.

And he doesn't look back.

CALEB

I WAS A FOOL FOR LOVE.

All my pride, all my great promises, they came to nothing. Tempted by the innocent promise in her eyes. Seduced by the wanton gasps of her passion, the fever of owning her supple flesh.

They say all that glitters is not gold, but her lies gleamed bright enough to dazzle even my jaded eye.

I thought she could be my salvation. The one pure thing in the midst of the charlatans and vipers. The sweet sin of her body made me forget myself. My rules. My control.

But not any longer.

The haze of desire has lifted, and I see the truth behind her seduction. Because none of it was real. All those deceitful nights. Every last whispered sin.

I wanted her enough to risk everything.

Now I desire only one thing.

Her ruin.

TO BE CONTINUED...

Juliet and Caleb's wild love story continues in the next book in the series, Flawless Ruin - available to order now!

FLAWLESS: BOOK TWO
FLAWLESS RUIN

How far will you go for desire? **Discover the next installment of the sensual, thrilling saga from USA Today bestselling author Roxy Sloane.**

She consumed me, body and soul. And now I'll pay the price for my weakness.

But so will she.

Her words may be false, but her body can't lie. Desire is the one true thing left between us, still binding our fates. A chain. A curse.

A weapon.

Desire was my undoing, but now?

Desire will be her *ruin*.

Roxy Sloane is a USA Today bestselling author, with over 2 million books sold world-wide. Roxy loves indulging her naughty side by writing sinful erotica that pushes the limits. She lives in Los Angeles, and enjoys shocking whoever looks at her laptop screen when she writes in local coffee shops.

∾

To get free books, news and more, CLICK HERE to sign up to my VIP list!

∾

www.roxysloane.com
roxy@roxysloane.com

Printed in Great Britain
by Amazon

79808022R00129